Jose's Farm Adventure

The Cow Boss Series

By Karen Kasper

Illustrations by Jane Engel

Halo ● ●●●
Publishing International

Karen Kasper

ISBN 13: 978-1-61244-460-4
Library of Congress Control Number: 2016909534

Printed in the United States of America

www.halopublishing.com

Published by Halo Publishing International
1100 NW Loop 410
Suite 700 - 176
San Antonio, Texas 78213
Toll Free 1-877-705-9647
www.halopublishing.com
www.holapublishing.com
e-mail: contact@halopublishing.com

This book is dedicated to my daughters for their inspiration and editing advice. Also to my parents whose financial support is greatly appreciated.

Special thanks to my friend, Jane of Pleasant Achers of Hope. Her life-like illustrations are a true compliment to this little farm book.

"Beep, beep, beep," screams Jose's alarm clock. Jose stretches; he is excited to get up early today. He is going to work on the dairy farm with Mama and Papa. Jose remembers his boots and coveralls.

4

Papa parks the truck by the barn. Jose sees Charlie, the farm dog. When Papa turns the barn lights on, little kittens scamper out from behind the door.

The farm is very quiet this early in the morning. The only sound is cock-a-doodle-doo. Jose is startled but Papa explains that is a rooster crowing. His job is to wake up the farmers and all the farm animals. Jose grins because he thinks that is funny! He says, "Papa we should get a rooster!"

Papa warms milk for the calves. Jose helps Papa fill the bottles and put the nipples on. The rest of the milk is poured into large buckets for the older calves.

Jose is excited to ride with Papa on the little tractor. Charlie hops on to ride along. Mama rides in the back of the cart.

Moo, moo, moo say the calves when they hear the tractor coming.
Jose screeches "Hurry Papa, they are hungry!"

Papa shows Jose which calves get bottles. Jose laughs
when the calves stick out their tongue to get more milk
and to lick on him. Their tongue feels like sandpaper.

Jose asks Papa about the different color calves. Papa explains that the black and white calves are Holsteins while the brown calves are Jerseys.

Jose notices that the bigger calves drink their milk from a bucket. Papa explains that newborn calves drink from a bottle. After a month, they are trained to drink their milk from a bucket.

Charlie likes to help with calf chores too. He sneaks a drink of milk whenever he can. Jose tells Charlie to sit in Spanish, "Siéntate", Charlie obeys. Jose thinks it is funny that Charlie understands English and Spanish.

The little kittens gather around the cart, anxiously waiting for some spilled milk too. Jose wants to pick up every kitten. Their soft fur tickles his cheek and their tongues are like sandpaper too.

14

After the calves drink their milk, Papa and Jose feed them protein and corn.

The calves loudly crunch on their pellets all day. Ducks gather close by, patiently waiting for Papa to feed them corn.

It's time to wash all the bottles and buckets so they're clean for the next feeding. Jose dumps a lot of soap in the sink. Mama gasps as bubbles flow everywhere. Jose says, "Oops!"

Jose is amazed by the giant bales. He wonders why some are green and others are yellow. Papa explains that straw is yellow and is for the animals to sleep on. Hay is green which is used for cow feed. Jose chuckled when he saw Charlie and the puppies jumping back and forth on top of the giant bales.

Papa and Jose put straw into the calf pens. The calves joyfully jump around and then snuggle into the soft, clean bed. Jose is itchy and he discovers straw in his hair and inside his boots.

18

Jose peeks around the door, into the milking parlor. WOW, a giant cow.
He wonders if the brown cows give white milk too. Papa explains that all
milk is white. Jose likes to add chocolate to his glass of milk sometimes.

While the cows are in the parlor getting milked, Papa cleans the cow beds. He puts new straw on top to keep them dry and cozy.

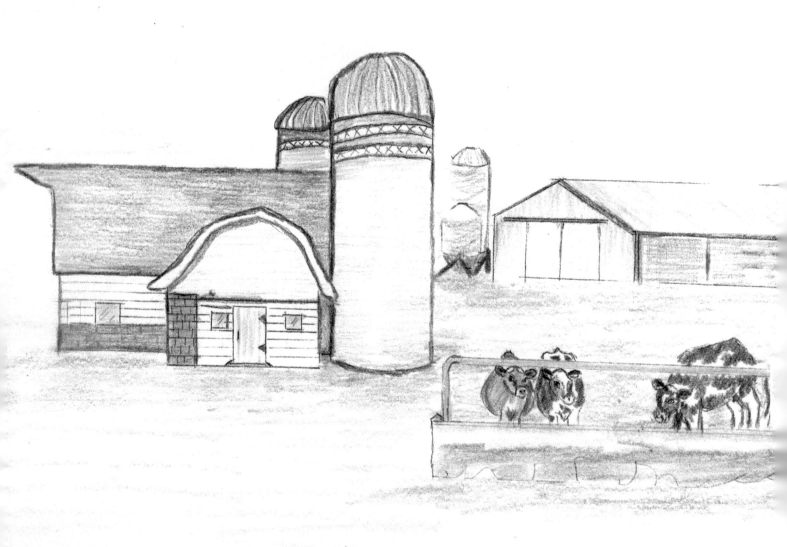

Farmer Pete is mixing feed for the cows. He uses a recipe to mix the protein, corn silage and hay. Papa explained that feed must provide the right nutrients for the cows to stay healthy.

Jose can't believe how big the feed mixing wagon is. He asks Papa "how much food does a cow eat every day?" Papa answered, "A whole bathtub full."

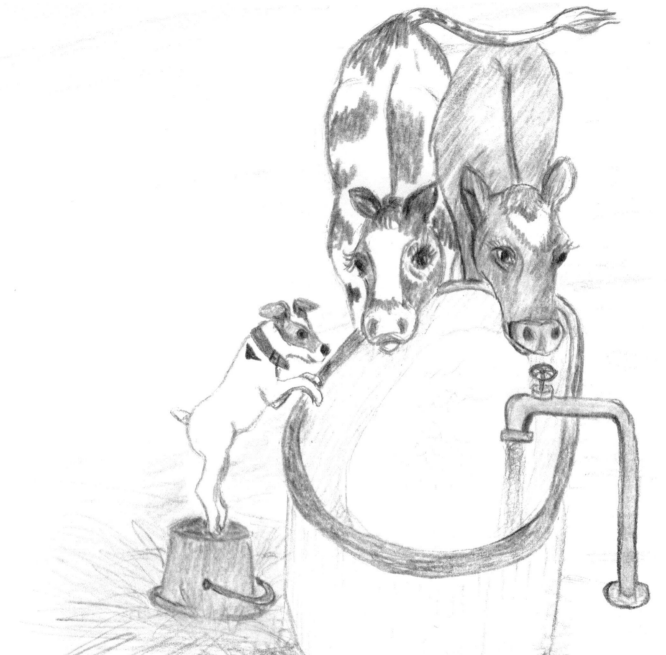

Cows also need fresh water every day. Jose was curious about exactly how much. Papa said, "Well when you like to fill the bathtub full to pretend you're swimming, that's how much water a cow drinks every day." Jose responded, "Wow that would make my tummy so full!"

After milking, the cows hurry back to the barn to find fresh food, clean beds and plenty of water. Jose said "When do the cows sleep?" Papa told him they sleep whenever they want to go lay down. Jose got a sly look on his face and replied, "I wish I was a cow!" Mama and Papa laughed so loud.

24

Jose, Papa and Mama had a busy day feeding the animals, giving them straw bedding and washing bottles and buckets.

Jose and Charlie were both sad when it was time to say good bye. Jose said "I don't want to go home; I will miss Charlie and all the animals." Papa promised Jose that he could visit the farm again.

EDGY
Embroidery

TRANSFORM CONVENTIONAL STITCHES INTO 25
UNCONVENTIONAL DESIGNS

RENEE ROMINGER

OWNER OF MOONRISE WHIMS

PAGE STREET
PUBLISHING CO.

PAGE STREET
PUBLISHING CO.

First published in 2017 by
Page Street Publishing Co.
27 Congress Street, Suite 105
Salem, MA 01970
www.pagestreetpublishing.com

Distributed by Macmillan, sales in Canada by The Canadian Manda Group.

21   20   19   18   17   1   2   3   4   5

ISBN-13: 978-1-62414-441-7

ISBN-10: 1-62414-441-1

Library of Congress Control Number: 2017933699

Cover and book design by Page Street Publishing Co.

Photography by Maria Jung Ibbitson

Printed and bound in China

As a member of 1% for the Planet, Page Street Publishing protects our planet by donating to nonprofits like The Trustees, which focuses on local land conservation. Learn more at onepercentfortheplanet.org.

DEDICATED, WITH LOVE, TO MY FAMILY AND FRIENDS
FOR THEIR SUPPORT AND ENCOURAGEMENT.

AND TO YOU, DEAR READER. MAY YOUR STITCHES BE CLEAN
AND PROJECTS TURN OUT SUPER BITCHIN'.

Contents

INTRODUCTION

Here's the deal: Embroidery is intimidating.

My goal is to make embroidery easy and approachable for everyone. I know what it's like to feel like you should know everything or as though there is a "right" and "wrong" way. It's easy to become overwhelmed before you even create your first stitch.

Maybe we feel intimidated by embroidery because of its long history. We're still stitching the same way our ancestors did centuries ago all over the world. However, the notion that you have to have an encyclopedic knowledge of every skill or stitch out there to create beautiful art deserves to stay in the past as well.

There is more than one way to create several kinds of stitches, and you may find that the traditional way, rules and "supposed to's" just don't fit you. They didn't fit me, either. I don't believe that we need to overcomplicate embroidery, so I do things a little bit differently.

I'd classify my style as "modern edgy." I love to work with juxtaposition, taking strong elements and mixing them with delicate florals or adding some sass to a pretty design. I especially love a modern twist on a vintage classic. These patterns have various other inspiration points as well, rooted in classic tales, science fiction and tattoo styles. They're made with dreamy inspiration so you can ascribe your own meaning and stories to them. You'll find everything here from classic floral beauties to carved human skulls.

What makes this so badass is taking a classic medium like embroidery and doing whatever the hell we want with it. It doesn't always have to be a pleasant "Home Sweet Home," and you don't have to follow the rules. You can be as weird as you want to be.

Throughout this book I'll be sharing my tips and tricks with you so when you dive into the often murky waters of embroidery, you'll feel confident, prepared and empowered to do things your own way, too.

I've laid out at least one project specifically for each stitch that I'll be teaching you. As you work your way through and the projects become more complex, I'll be incorporating more stitches and techniques. With each pattern, I've broken down the smartest way to tackle it. I encourage you to get creative with the patterns if you feel like switching up the fabric, floss colors or text.

My number one piece of advice for beginners is the most timeless and boring of all: practice! I encourage you to practice each stitch on a scrap piece of fabric before you move on to the pattern so you have the movement and skill down, especially if you are new to embroidery. This is the way I learned a long time ago, and it builds up your confidence so you're less likely to get frustrated with a stitch or pattern when it's all very new to you. Even if it takes you an hour of practice to finally create a rose that you're happy with, you'll keep that skill for a lifetime.

When a lot of the world feels like screens and constant rushing around in a daze, there's just something about creating a tangible item with your hands. Take some time out of your day, whether it's twenty minutes or a few hours, to sit back, relax, grab yourself a cup of tea (or whiskey) and stitch something amazing. You'll be so amazed at what your hands can create.

Ready to kick some embroidery ass?

Renee Rominger

GETTING STARTED

HOW TO HOOP FABRIC

Actually getting your fabric in the hoop can be a little bit frustrating, but it's important to take your time. For information on selecting fabric, see page 94. If it's too loose or taut, all the time you spent stitching carefully may be for nothing as the end result could be warped by the fabric tension.

1. To begin, separate your hoop by unscrewing it at the top. You'll now have two pieces—the inner ring and the outer ring with the screw at the top.

2. For your fabric, cut a square length large enough to fit the hoop with at least an inch of space left. For instance, a 5-inch (13-cm) round hoop would need at least a 7-inch (18-cm) square of fabric.

3. Take your inner ring and lay it flat against a clean, hard surface, then place your fabric square over it. This next part may seem small but it's very important when it comes to your finished piece looking as clean and neat as possible.

   Take a close look at your fabric. You'll notice a horizontal and vertical weave pattern to it. When you place it over your inner hoop circle, imagine where the screw top will be when you lay the top ring. That is your "north" now.

   Align the fabric evenly in the center, with the weave oriented vertically to that spot. Place the adjustable outer ring on top. Tighten it slightly so that it isn't slipping around.

4. If your fabric is aligned properly, this next step should be easy. The trick to an even stretch is to start gently pulling the fabric from the back, beginning with the right side, then the left. At this point, you're not pulling very tight, just enough to get rid of any looseness. Next, gently pull the bottom, then the top. Be gentle and patient once you get to the top section, since the adjustable screw can tug on the fabric.

5. Next, repeat this process, pulling a little bit more now until the fabric is nice and taut. If you've done it correctly, the weave pattern in the fabric should not be too distorted. Inevitably, some parts may be a little wonky, but that's okay. The goal is not to have any loose areas or have it be so tight that it could double as a drum.

6. Lastly, remove any excess fabric so it doesn't get in your way. I always cut around the edge so the excess fabric follows the line of the hoop, with at least 1 inch (2.5 cm) left.

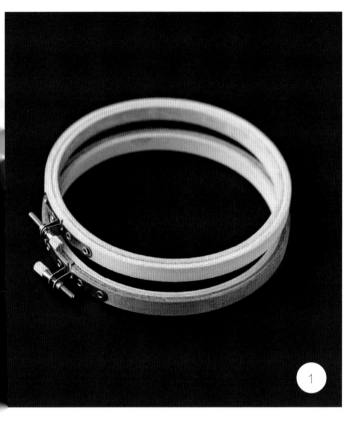

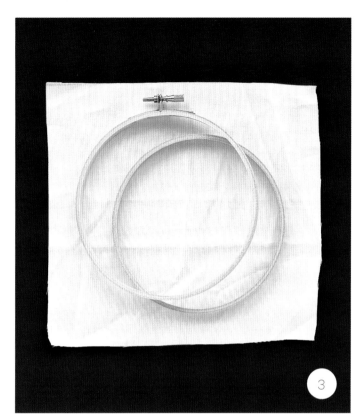

As you work you may find that you like a tighter surface or a looser one. If it's comfortable for you and doesn't mess up your stitches, feel free to modify as you see fit.

If you're using a fabric that has any stretch to it, you may have difficulty hooping it. It's not impossible to work with, but depending on how much stretch there is to it, it may be a pain. You also run the risk of overstretching, which would result in it springing back once you remove the hoop, which spells disaster for your stitches.

PATTERN TRANSFER

My preferred method of transferring a pattern, and what I'll be teaching, involves some creative processes but I swear by it both for the simplicity and ease of it. It involves hooping your fabric "backward" and then tracing your pattern onto it.

First, we have to hoop our fabric "backward." We achieve this by simply turning the fabric over when we hoop it regularly. Now, the face of your fabric is technically in the back and will lay wonderfully flat against your pattern. Select a pattern (page 105). After you trace your pattern, you can stitch it this way or remove the fabric and rehoop it the right way out.

Tracing the pattern onto your fabric is as simple as it sounds. Using whichever pen, pencil or marker you've chosen to mark your fabric with (pge 92), trace the design directly onto your fabric.

Depending on your fabric, sometimes you won't need any source of backlight to see your pattern. However, having a light source to illuminate from the back makes this task easier and less frustrating as you can clearly see your pattern. If you're using dark fabric, you will absolutely need backlight.

There are tools made specifically for tracing called light boxes or light boards. While they're handy and made specifically for this task, they're not necessary.

If you've got a window and some sun in your home, you're good to go. I recommend gently taping the pattern onto the window (washi tape is great for this—it's very gentle and won't leave residue on your windows), then laying your "backward hoop" flat against it to trace it. Make sure you place it in a comfortable position so you're not straining yourself.

Alternatively, if you don't have access to a light box or sunny window, you can get creative with a computer, laptop, tablet or TV. Chances are you've got some electronic devices that emanate light from a hard, flat surface. I used an old tablet as a "light box" for years.

Try not to overthink this too much. Maybe it looks or feels a little silly tracing from a window or even a laptop, but it's a quick and easy task.

HOW TO THREAD A NEEDLE

1. After you've learned how to pick the proper tools for embroidery (page 89), it's time to get more familiar with them. The first step is to thread your needle in preparation for your first stitch. First, cut a length of floss. It should be shorter than the length of your arm, or about 20 inches (50 cm). Use sharp scissors to get a clean, even and unfrayed cut to make threading it through easy as pie.

2. Hold the floss between the thumb and pointer finger of your dominant hand and hold the needle in the other. If you're using the proper embroidery needle, you should have no problem bringing the floss end through the eye. Pull the floss through the needle about 5 inches (13 cm). This length will keep the floss secured in the needle as you work. On the opposite end, tie a simple knot. This will be what stops your thread from coming through the fabric with your first stitch.

HOW TO BEGIN A STITCH

Beginning any stitch starts with bringing the needle up from the back of your fabric. Pull gently until the knot at the end of the fabric stops the motion. Make sure your first stitches don't pull too tightly so you don't pucker the fabric.

HOW TO END A STITCH

For most projects, you'll have to end a stitch in the middle of a project several times to rethread a new piece of floss and resume work.

To make an end knot easy, make sure you leave at least 5 inches (13 cm) of thread. Working until it's nearly gone is tempting but can make the end knot difficult, if not impossible, and too loose.

On your last stitch with this length of floss, unthread your needle and set it aside. Lay your hoop flat, with the back of it facing you. Your goal is to have the knot lie flat against the fabric so your last stitch doesn't loosen. The trick to this is to start your knot as a large loop. Slide the knot down and gently pull, holding it to the fabric until it's tight. Cut the excess thread off, leaving only about a ¼-inch (0.6-cm) length.

BEGINNING YOUR NEXT STITCH WITH A NEW LENGTH OF FLOSS

When you've completed a length of floss and are beginning again with a new one, simply continue on as though it's the original length of thread. For the first stitch or two, be careful not to accidentally pierce through either your beginning or ending knots.

STRANDS OF FLOSS

Embroidery floss is made from six individual cotton strands gently twisted together. Most of the time, all six strands are used, but you can easily separate the strands and use anywhere from one to five for smaller details.

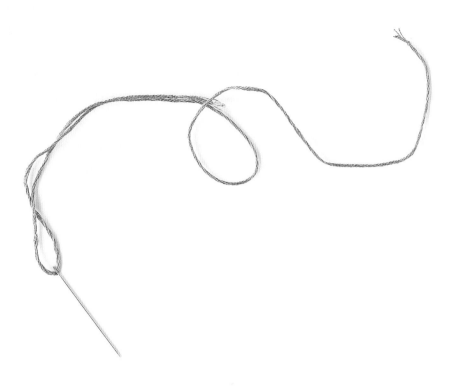

1

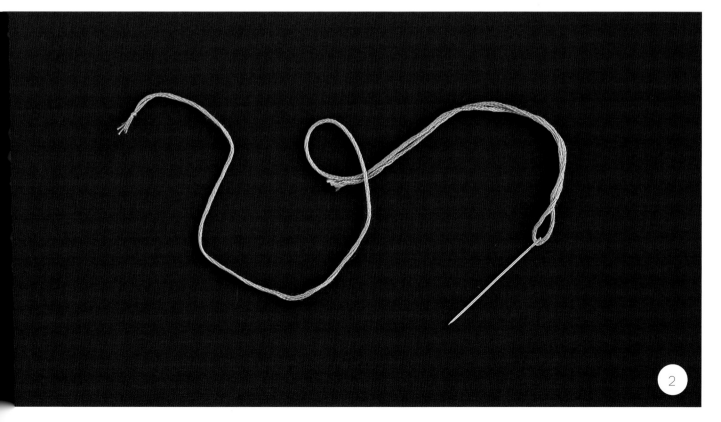

2

two

BACK STITCH

The back stitch is by far the most useful stitch you will ever learn. Because of its simplicity and diversity, it can feasibly be used for nearly everything. However, it's important to take your time to learn to do it properly for happy, clean stitches. As you learn and stitch, pay attention to your stitch lengths so that they are even and meet together as seamlessly as possible.

One single wonky stitch can throw off the look of your final project, so if it looks off, take a second to set your needle aside, gently take out the last stitch or two and redo them.

For the back stitch, we'll be using the stab technique, meaning that you pull your needle and thread all the way through with each step. Follow the lines of the pattern as if you were tracing them. When you come to a curve or turn in your pattern, begin to shorten your stitches so the curve doesn't look boxy.

1. Bring your threaded needle up and through point A. Bring your needle down and through point B. This is your first completed stitch. Except for shortening your stitches when you navigate curves, all of your stitches should be approximately the same length as this one.

2. Your second stitch here is where we start working "back." Bring your needle up and through point C.

3. Bring your needle down and through point B. This is where you want to pay close attention. Make sure that your needle is coming down through the same hole as point B. If you accidentally create a new hole slightly to the side, your stitches will look off.

4. Repeat this motion again, bringing your needle up and through point D, then back down through point C.

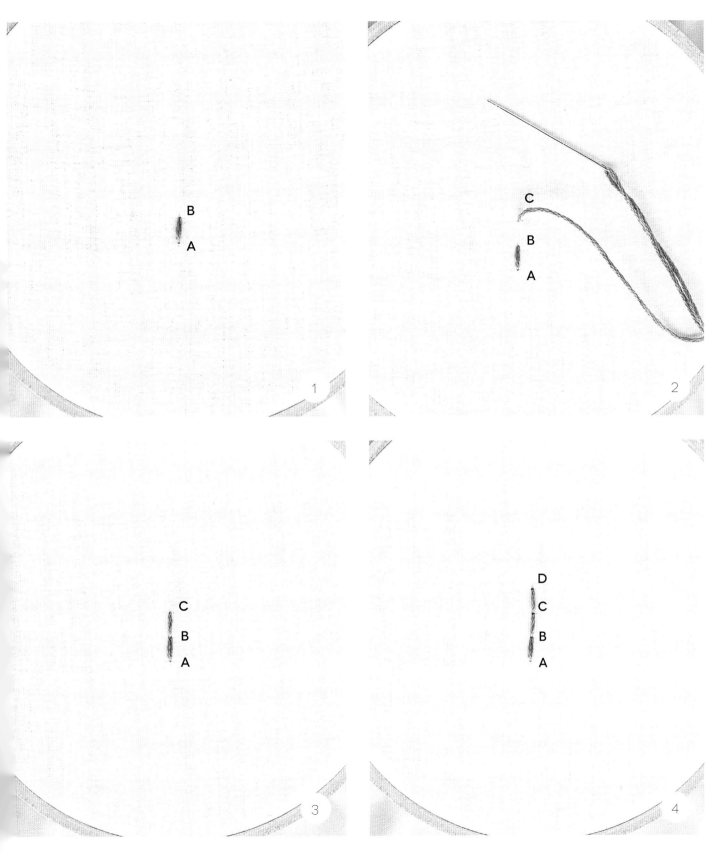

POISON BOTTLE

Our first project is inspired by the various lovely glass bottles that you'd find in a dusty old apothecary. It has a beautiful crystal stopper and swirly decorative label in a dreamy color palette. Drink at your own risk, however. This medicine is a little harsh.

PATTERN USED: page 105

STITCH USED: Back stitch (page 14)

HOOP SIZE: 6″ (15-cm) round

FABRIC COLOR SHOWN: Purple

COLOR PALETTE

BOTTLE AND STOPPER: Dusty purple

STOPPER BASE: Gray

LIQUID: Light purple

LABEL: Light blue

LINES: Metallic gold

Transfer the pattern to the fabric.

Begin first with the bottle. Using all six strands of floss, start at the top and work your way down. When you get to the crystal bottle stopper, I suggest using long, clean lines rather than a series of shorter stitches. Finish with the text and designs on the inside of the label; split your thread in half and use only three strands.

ANATOMICAL HEART

This design is inspired by the anatomy sketches that you'd likely find in a 100-year-old medical textbook. What I love about the heart, and what I think draws people to it, is how it is both so human as well as emotional. It's amazing to see the intricacy of this vital organ that beats in all of us, which we associate so strongly with love.

PATTERN USED: page 107

STITCH USED: Back stitch (page 14)

HOOP SIZE: 7" (18-cm) round

FABRIC COLOR SHOWN: Cream

COLOR PALETTE: Deep red

Transfer the pattern to the fabric.

The anatomical heart pattern has a lot of curves and turns, so make sure to shorten your stitches as you go so your lines don't look boxy or sharp. The example photo is on a cream-colored fabric, but this would also look great on a beautiful patterned fabric. We'll be using all six strands of thread for this piece.

I suggest working from the outside in, first outlining your heart, then coming back to fill in the details, leaving the veins for last. When you begin on the veins, you'll notice that the main one down the middle is thicker than the others. To get this effect, first back stitch the vein as you would normally, then back stitch right next to it to thicken the line.

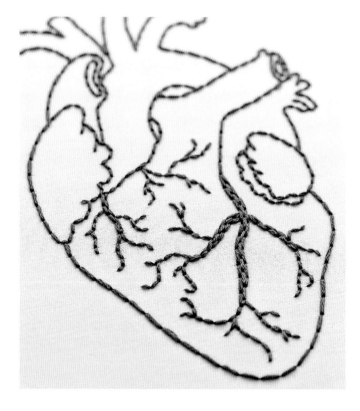

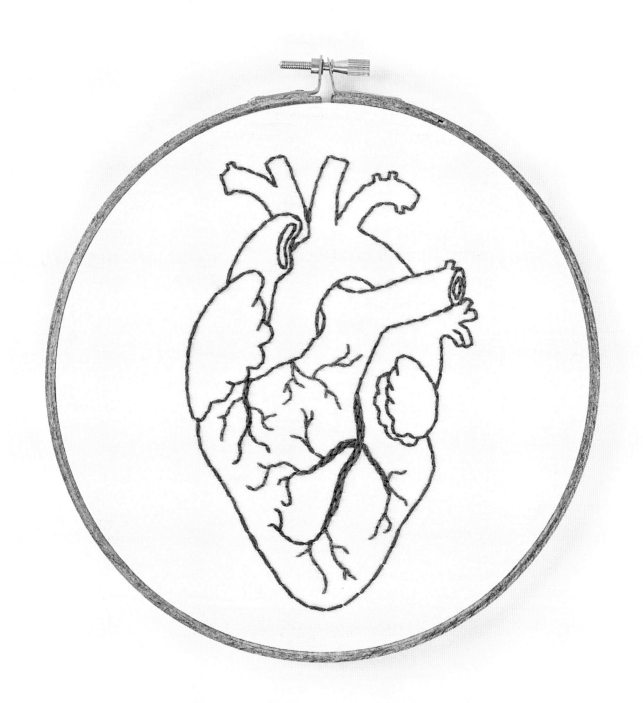

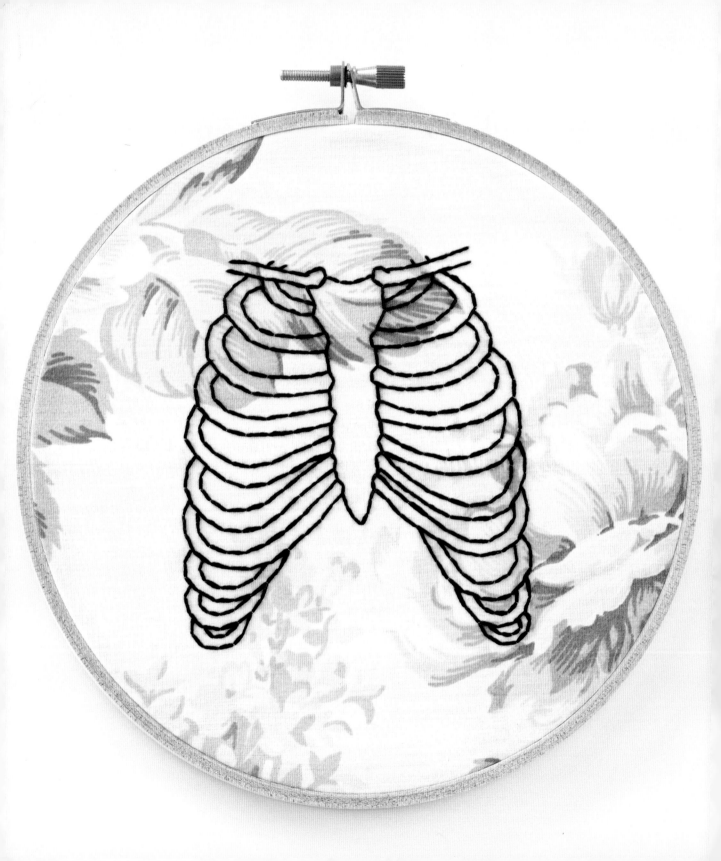

RIB CAGE

This rib cage pattern is a play on one of my favorite things that inspires me the most—juxtaposition. I love mixing macabre items with soft florals. In this case I've paired a beautiful rib cage outline in stark black with a lovely vintage floral fabric.

PATTERN USED: page 109

STITCH USED: Back stitch (page 14)

HOOP SIZE: 6" (15-cm) round

FABRIC COLOR SHOWN: Floral print

COLOR PALETTE: Black

Transfer the pattern to the fabric.

This is a very straightforward pattern. Because there are some smaller details, we'll be using only three strands of floss so the lines are clean. I suggest stitching the sternum first so you have a center to work from. Starting from either the left or right side, work your way down, stitching the outside of each rib, then the inside. Regarding fabric, any light pattern works great here, but you could use a solid-color fabric as well.

HAUNTED HOUSE ON THE HILL

This haunted house on the hill is reminiscent of old ghost stories. The mysterious centuries-old home sits up high on a hill among the moon and stars, far from town. The only movement anyone ever sees is a new headstone in the yard. Is it really haunted? Or is it all in our heads?

PATTERN USED: page 111

STITCH USED: Back stitch (page 14)

HOOP SIZE: 6" (15-cm) round

FABRIC COLOR SHOWN: Cream

COLOR PALETTE

HOUSE AND MOON: Black

STARS: Gold

Transfer the pattern to the fabric.

For the haunted house outline and roof, instead of using a series of short back stitches to create the lines, we'll stitch them as one long line. This will make the lines clean and sharp. Make sure you have good tension in your fabric and hoop so the stitches don't loosen.

The pattern will be using only three strands of floss to keep the lines thin and fine. I suggest beginning first on the outline of the house, then working your way in to fill in the details. To add the stars, use three strands of gold floss and back stitch to overlap three stitches.

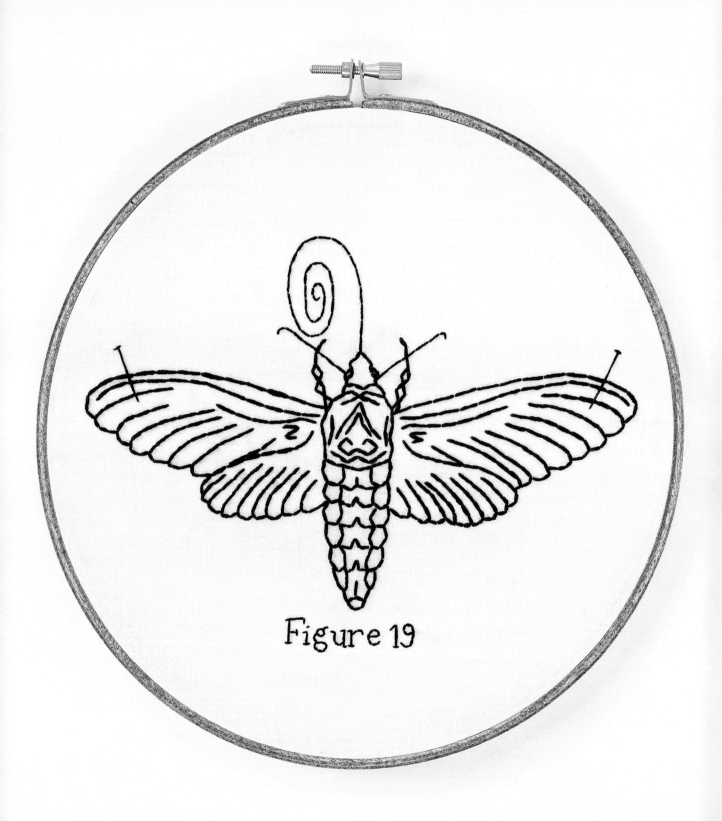

Figure 19

MOTH

This delicate moth with his large, dusty wings is inspired by what you'd find in an old museum. It's beautiful but also, when you notice the pins holding his wings down, a little grotesque. Either way, he's an impressive specimen.

PATTERN USED: page 113

STITCH USED: Back stitch (page 14)

HOOP SIZE: 8" (20-cm) round

FABRIC COLOR SHOWN: Cream

COLOR PALETTE: Black

Transfer the pattern to the fabric.

This moth project is a great exercise in stitching curves and details. Remember to shorten your stitches as you come around curves and turns so the design doesn't look boxy or sharp. I suggest starting on the body of your moth beginning on the outside and working your way in. For the center body, head, wings and lines in the wings, use all six strands of floss.

When you're finished with those, split your floss in half, using only three strands to stitch up the antennae, pins and text. Using fewer strands will give you a thinner and more detailed look as well as add dimension to your design.

three

SATIN STITCH

Now that you've learned the back stitch, satin stitch should be a breeze. Think of it as a series of long back stitches. I love how "satin stitch" evokes a smooth and silky image. Similarly, so should your stitches when done correctly. Using this technique creates beautiful work with a filled-in look. It makes designs pop and adds texture.

The trick here is even stitches. The way I achieve that, and will be teaching you as well, is by using what I call guidelines and starting in the middle of a design rather than the top or bottom. This method gives you greater control and your end product will be much nicer.

Satin stitch is also very versatile. You'll see how it's similar to the leaves stitch (page 52) and how it can be used for small details in later patterns.

We'll be using the stab technique for the satin stitch, moving the needle and thread all the way through with each step. In this example and in the patterns, we'll be using the outer lines as our start and end points and the guidelines to keep our stitches straight and even.

1. Bring your threaded needle up through point A and down through point B. Make sure your first stitch here is even and straight as it will be the base and guide for the rest.

2. Come back around to the right side and bring your needle up and through point C. This should be very close to point A so that when you continue this stitch, no fabric shows through. Take your time when working near your first stitch so you don't accidentally snag your beginning knot on the underside of your fabric.

3. Bring your needle down through point D, also very close to point B and parallel to point A to B.

4. Continue working right to left as you work your way down. Make sure you start and end your stitches as close to the lines of your pattern as you can.

5. Once this half is complete, start working your way upward, beginning with point E to F.

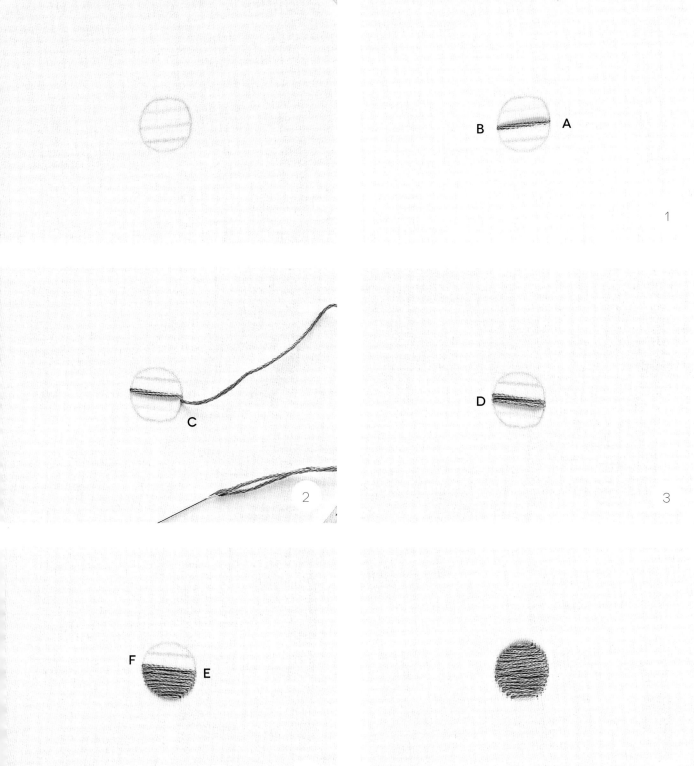

SHARP TEETH

My, what sharp teeth you have! This design is inspired by classic tales of the undead and is another juxtaposition as we pair the lovely deep red lips with some very sharp fangs.

PATTERN USED: page 115

STITCHES USED: Satin stitch (page 26), back stitch (page 14)

HOOP SIZE: 6" (15-cm) round

FABRIC COLOR SHOWN: Cream

COLOR PALETTE

LIPS: Dark red

TEETH: Black

Transfer the pattern to the fabric.

The lips in this pattern use a lot of floss. Before you begin, make sure you have at least two skeins of your lipstick color so you don't run out.

For this pattern, I suggest first starting with the lips, using satin stitch and all six strands of floss. Make sure you have a nice tension in your hoop so the longer stitches don't become loose as you work.

Finish up with the teeth by using only three strands of the black floss and using a back stitch. When you come to the fangs, I suggest using one single long back stitch for each side so you get a nice point to them.

Want your design to have a little extra bite? Not only can you play around with the lipstick colors, but you can add your own text on the inside of the mouth.

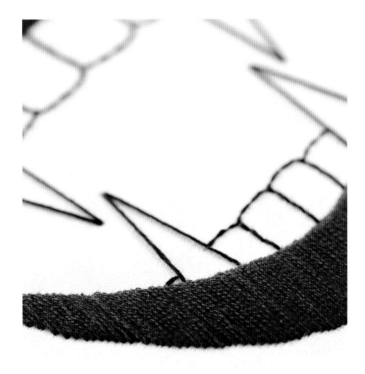

OUTER SPACE

With this pattern, we venture out into the vastness and cold dark of space. We travel past new planets and star systems, into the great unknown.

PATTERN USED: page 117

STITCHES USED: Satin stitch (page 26), back stitch (page 14), French knot (page 56)

HOOP SIZE: 5" (13-cm) round

FABRIC COLOR SHOWN: Black

COLOR PALETTE

PLANET 1: Green blue

PLANET 2: Light blue (primary), medium blue (secondary)

PLANET 3: Dusty purple (primary), medium purple (secondary)

PLANET 4: Light orange (primary), peach (secondary)

PLANET 4 RING: Dark peach

STARS AND GALAXY: Gold

Transfer the pattern to the fabric.

This pattern looks best on dark fabric, so make sure you have the right marking tools for your fabric before you begin (page 92). We'll be using all six strands of floss for the satin stitch planets and the ring around planet 4.

Begin with planet 1 on the top left since it's only one color. Moving on to the planet below it, planet 2, use the primary color to stitch it completely. Come back in with the secondary color to add lines over your existing stitches to give it some personality. Continue this same effect with the other two-color planet on the top right, planet 3, and planet 4 on the bottom right.

To create the ring around planet 4, use one long back stitch across the body of the planet to connect your ring from right to left, rather than piercing the satin stitch with shorter stitches.

Next, thread your needle with three strands of gold floss. Use back stitch to create the galaxy. For the small stars, use very short back stitches. Using the French knot technique, stitch the shooting stars. Alternately, you can use a single back stitch.

For the shooting star tails and larger stars, thread only a single strand of gold floss. Use three back stitches for the tails. To complete your project, overlap three back stitches for the larger stars.

DON'T BE A PRICK

Do you have a black thumb like me? Thankfully, this prickly pair of beautiful cacti in a dusty vintage desert–inspired color palette can't be killed, no matter how hard you try.

PATTERN USED: page 119

STITCH USED: Satin stitch (page 26), back stitch (page 14)

HOOP SIZE: 5" (13-cm) round

FABRIC COLOR SHOWN: Cream

COLOR PALETTE

VASE: Dusty light peach, dusty light blue

CIRCLE CACTUS: Light blue green

TALL CACTUS: Light green

NEEDLES: White

TEXT: Dark green

Transfer the pattern to the fabric.

This pattern contains a lot of satin stitch, so it is a great practice piece and example of how to use it in different ways. Use all six strands of your floss for all of the satin stitching. I suggest starting with your pot, then moving to the short cactus in front, then finishing with the tall cactus in the back.

Once your plants are completed, if you want to add some needles, thread a single strand of white embroidery floss and stitch straight lines that cross down the seams of your stitches as seen in the example.

Finish up with the text, using back stitch and three strands of the dark green floss.

GEOMETRIC SUCCULENT TERRARIUM

This pattern is again for other black thumbs like me who can't keep a plant alive. This spiky two-tone succulent looks clean and modern in its beautiful gold geometric terrarium.

PATTERN USED: page 121

STITCHES USED: Satin stitch (page 26), back stitch (page 14)

HOOP SIZE: 6" (15-cm) round

FABRIC COLOR SHOWN: Cream

COLOR PALETTE

DIRT: Dark brown (primary), dark cocoa brown (secondary)

LEAVES: Medium green, light green

TERRARIUM: Gold

Transfer the pattern to the fabric.

This will be a more challenging project because we'll be using a lot of satin stitch techniques and colors. The pattern is a great example of how you can use satin stitch in different ways, with the dirt in the bottom of the terrarium being stitched at an angle and two-tone. We'll be using all 6 strands of the floss for the satin stitch. Leave the gold terrarium for last.

Begin by stitching the dirt in a diagonal pattern, using the lighter shade of brown first. Afterward, come back in with a few lines stitched using the darker shade of brown over your existing stitches.

Next, begin with the succulent. Start on the most up-front leaves, working your way back. Once you're done with your satin stitches, take a step back and look at them. If you notice any open spaces, go back and fill them in as needed.

For the terrarium, use all 6 strands of the metallic floss to make long, clean back stitches. Essentially, you want to connect the dots at the corners of the geometric pattern. Make sure the tension between your fabric and hoop is good since these will be long stitches and you don't want them to loosen too much or droop.

four

STEM STITCH

With the stem stitch, we're starting to branch out a little bit and get fancy. A well-done stem stitch will have a ropelike appearance and is softer looking than a back stitch. This makes it great in floral work and in curvy lettering. It does, as its namesake suggests, make some great stems.

I do my stem stitch a little different from how it's most often taught. Essentially, I do it backward. I've found that this gives me greater control and a more even and clean result. Learning this will be very similar to learning the motions of the back stitch.

We'll again be using the stab technique, pulling the needle and thread all the way through with each step, and you should follow the lines of the pattern as if you were tracing it. Try to keep your stitches uniform in length except when you come to curves and turns, as those should be gradually shortened to avoid any sharp points.

1. Bring your threaded needle up through point A and down through point B. This is the same as if you were beginning a back stitch, but keep in mind that this first stitch will be twice as long as the rest of your stitches.

2. Bring your needle up and through point C. This should be half the length of A to B.

3. Bring your needle down and through point D. Point D should be approximately halfway between point A and B and tucked under the stitch. This is the end of your "starting" stitches and the rest will be uniform.

4. Bring your needle up and through point E and down through point B, very similarly to how you would be doing a back stitch.

5. Continue this process until you come to the end of your pattern.

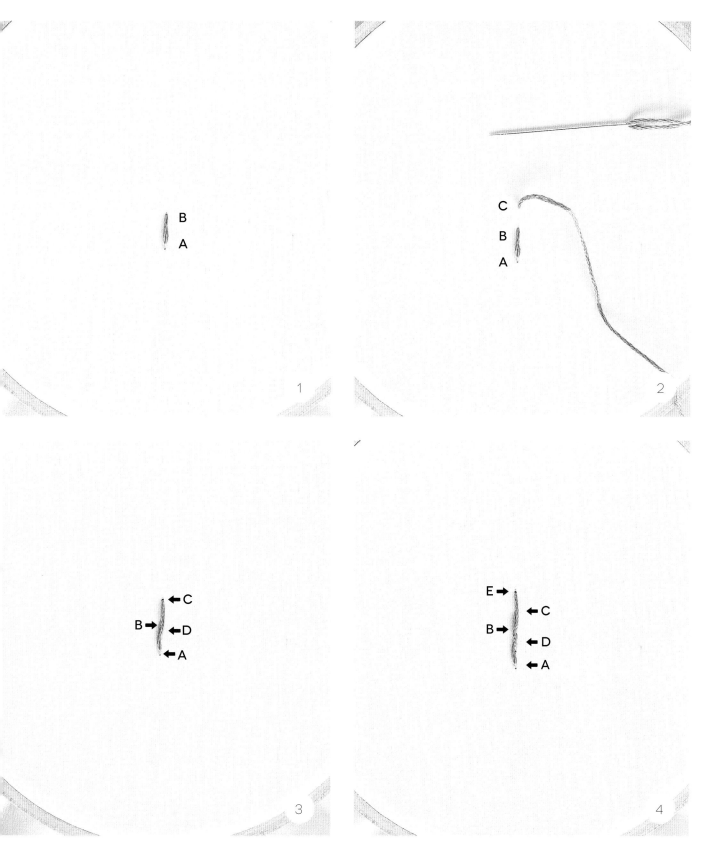

CANDY HEARTS

These colorful candy hearts are a little less sweet than the others. If you're feeling a little "meh" about this text, feel free to add your own sassy messages!

PATTERN USED: page 123

STITCHES USED: Stem stitch (page 36), back stitch (page 14)

HOOP SIZE: 6" (15-cm) round

FABRIC COLOR SHOWN: Pink

COLOR PALETTE
UGH HEART: Bright purple

MEH HEART: Bright blue

TEXT: White

Transfer the pattern to the fabric.

The candy heart design is very simple but very customizable. You can follow the pattern examples or switch up the colors of the thread and fabric. Use all 6 strands of floss for every stitch in this pattern. Begin first with the heart in the front, then the heart in the back, using stem stitch. Save the text for last, using back stitch.

CRYSTAL BALL

What's in your future? This mystical crystal ball is swirling with ideas. The dreamy color palette and design evoke an image of a trip to a mysterious fortune-teller's tent. If you really want to challenge your creativity, create your own fortune by filling in the crystal ball with your own design!

PATTERN USED: page 125

STITCHES USED: Stem stitch (page 36), back stitch (page 14), French knot (page 56)

HOOP SIZE: 6" (15-cm) round

FABRIC COLOR SHOWN: Purple

COLOR PALETTE

GLASS: Light gray

BASE OUTLINE: Mocha brown

BASE DESIGN: Gray purple

MOON: Light blue

SWIRLS: Light gray purple

STARS AND LINES: Gold

Transfer the pattern to the fabric.

For this pattern we'll be using primarily stem stitch, except for the straight lines surrounding the crystal ball and the stars, which will use back stitch. There is a small French knot detail on the base of the crystal ball. If you'd like, you can use a small back stitch instead. Use all 6 strands of floss for each stitch.

Begin first with the crystal ball and base, working your way inward to the detail work, then finishing with the single back stitch details on the outside.

CAN U NOT BANNER HEART

This banner heart is perfect for when you're just a little bit over it. Inspired by a classic tattoo style, it's also ready for your own sassy custom text!

PATTERN USED: page 127

STITCHES USED: Stem stitch (page 36), back stitch (page 14)

HOOP SIZE: 5" (13-cm) round

FABRIC COLOR SHOWN: Cream

COLOR PALETTE

BANNER AND TEXT: Black

HEART: Deep red

Transfer the pattern to the fabric.

This pattern will be using primarily stem stitch with some back stitch for details that need sharp, clean lines. Begin by using all six strands of your floss and stem stitch your heart, then the banner. Using all six strands of floss, use back stitch for the lettering.

Add your own text for an awesome custom piece!

GHOULS NIGHT OUT

This trio of sassy ghouls is ready for its night out! These ghouls have escaped the cemetery and are ready for some haunting fun.

PATTERN USED: page 129

STITCHES USED: Stem stitch (page 36), satin stitch (page 26), back stitch (page 14)

HOOP SIZE: 7" (18-cm) round

FABRIC COLOR SHOWN: Pink

COLOR PALETTE
GHOSTS: White

EYES: Black

HEART EYES: Light red

Transfer the pattern to the fabric.

This pattern is very straightforward and uses all six strands of floss for each element. I suggest first stitching up the bodies of the ghosts with stem stitch, then adding the face details. I've used satin stitch for the eyes and mouths in the example, but you're welcome to use a back stitch to outline those features instead. Use a back stitch for the winking eye.

NOPE, UGH, AS IF

This sassy trio is the perfect project to flex your stem stitch muscles. Stitch up one or all three. Want some extra credit? Make one with your own text!

PATTERN USED: page 131

STITCH USED: Stem stitch (page 36), French knot (page 56)

HOOP SIZE: 3" x 5" (8 x 13-cm) oval or a 5" (13-cm) round

FABRIC COLOR SHOWN: Floral pattern

COLOR PALETTE: Black

Transfer the pattern to the fabric.

I've used a vintage floral pattern for the example photos, but this is the perfect design to get creative with fabric choices. How cute would these look on a sassy cat fabric? Alternately, they'd look modern and adorable on a solid-color fabric.

This is the only project in the book that uses an oval hoop—they're difficult to find in stores, but I adore them. If you can't get your hands on one, in stores or online, this design fits perfectly in a 5-inch (13-cm) round hoop as well.

Oval hoops can be difficult to stitch in. Due to their odd shape, sometimes the inside and outer rings don't match up well, which leads to loose fabric that can be annoying to stitch on. If you run into this problem, stitch it first in a 5-inch (13-cm) round hoop, then transfer it to your 3 x 5-inch (8x13-cm) oval hoop to set.

This design is super simple to stitch up. Use all six strands of floss and stitch it in the direction you would as if you were writing. If you choose the "As if" design, I've used a French knot to dot the "i," but a single back stitch also works well here.

HOW DOES YOUR GARDEN GROW?

Learning to create beautiful greenery is a fantastic tool for embroidery. Don't underestimate the power of some leaves! I often find myself adding leaves and ferns when I want to add dimension, depth or more intrigue to my patterns. They look beautiful as a stand-alone feature or as an addition to patterns. For example, with the Fern Skull (page 51) pattern, you'll see how a simple fern stitch adds to a classic design.

FERN STITCH

The fern stitch creates a lovely and simple vine-and-leaf design that is great as a bookend to nearly any design needing a little sprucing up. It's also great incorporated into floral work.

We'll be using the stab technique, pulling the needle and thread all the way through with each step. In the step-by-step instructions and the pattern for the fern stitch project, I've drawn the pattern as the center vine as well as guidelines for the leaves. I don't use the guidelines when I do the fern stitch anymore, but I encourage you to use them while you learn so your leaves are even.

The fern stitch is similar to a back stitch with the addition of your leaves, which will all meet back into the same stitch.

1. Bring your threaded needle up and through point A and down through point B.

2. To begin your first leaf, bring your needle up and through point C, which will be slightly to the side. Bring it down and through point B.

3. Bring your needle up and through point D and down through point B.

4. To begin your next set, bring your needle up and through point E and down through A. Create your leaves by stitching F to A and G to A.

5. Repeat this process.

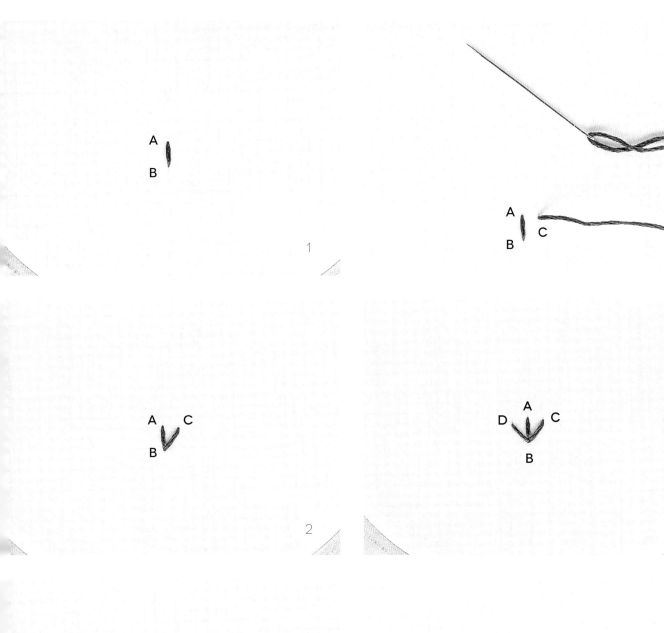

FERN SKULL

This pattern combines two of my favorite items: a classic skull and a fern border. It's a great example of how something clean and simple can be so effective. I've added interest by carving out a pattern on the forehead of the skull. This is also a perfect canvas for some creativity if you've got another pattern in mind for your skull.

PATTERN USED: **page 133**

STITCHES USED: **Fern stitch (page 48), back stitch (page 14)**

HOOP SIZE: **6" (15-cm) round**

FABRIC COLOR SHOWN: **Cream**

COLOR PALETTE

SKULL: **Black**

FERN: **Dark green**

Transfer the pattern to the fabric.

The main focal point of this design is the skull in the center. It's a good demonstration of how the simple and clean fern stitch works as a beautiful bookend to many embroidery designs.

First stitch up the skull using back stitch. Use all six strands of your floss to outline the skull, teeth, eyes and nose. Once those are completed, separate your floss into three strands to stitch the details, including all the cracks in the skull, the shading elements in the nose and eye, and the forehead carving. The shading uses long back stitches; make sure you have good tension between your hoop and fabric so the stitches don't loosen or sag.

Once you're happy with your skull, use the fern stitch for the leaves on the sides.

LEAVES

Leaves are beautiful on their own, make perfect filler for floral embroidery and are quick and easy once you get the hang of it. There are a lot of ways to stitch them, but I'll be teaching you my favorite way. The technique I use gives the leaves an almost 3D effect. I love a full-looking leaf; they're incredibly versatile. They can be as short, long, thin or fat as you wish.

Try out a few shapes and sizes as you learn.

We'll be using the stab technique to stitch up our leaves. This means with each step we'll be pulling the needle and thread all the way through with each stitch. They are very similar to both satin stitch and the back stitch. The pattern for leaves is the outline, which looks like a teardrop shape. We'll begin at the tip and work our way down. Follow the outside lines as you would with satin stitch.

As you stitch your leaves, keep in mind that the stitches will be more spread out toward the tip and taper in toward the base to create the teardrop shape of the leaf.

1. Bring your threaded needle up through point A and down and through point B. This first stitch is essentially the stem of your leaf, so make sure it's even and straight.

2. Bring your needle up through point C and down through point D.

3. Continue these steps down one side of your leaf with the stitches down to your base being more tapered and squished together. As you come to the last stitches on either side, they will be nearly perpendicular to your stem (A to B).

4. Continue this down the other side of your leaf.

   Optional last step: Use a short back stitch to attach a long stem to your finished leaf.

1

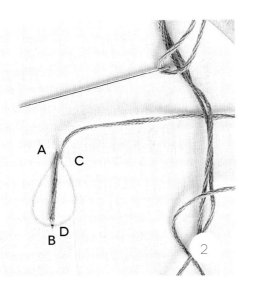

2

3

4

FALLING LEAVES

The Falling Leaves project is lovely in its simplicity and makes for fantastic leaf stitch practice, which will come in handy with floral embroidery. I've provided two color palettes and encourage you to create your own as well! These 4-inch (10-cm) hoop projects shine as part of a collection or as a minimalist decoration.

PATTERN USED: page 135

STITCHES USED: Leaf stitch (page 52)

HOOP SIZE: 4" (10-cm) round

FABRIC COLOR SHOWN: Cream

COLOR PALETTES

SPRING: Medium green, light green, light blue green, medium blue green

FALL: Burnt red orange, yellow, deep yellow, medium green

Transfer the pattern to the fabric.

This is a freeform pattern, so you can mimic the leaf colors in the example photo or choose them yourself organically as you work. The leaves pattern should be used as a guide for the general size and shape. If they don't match up exactly, that's okay.

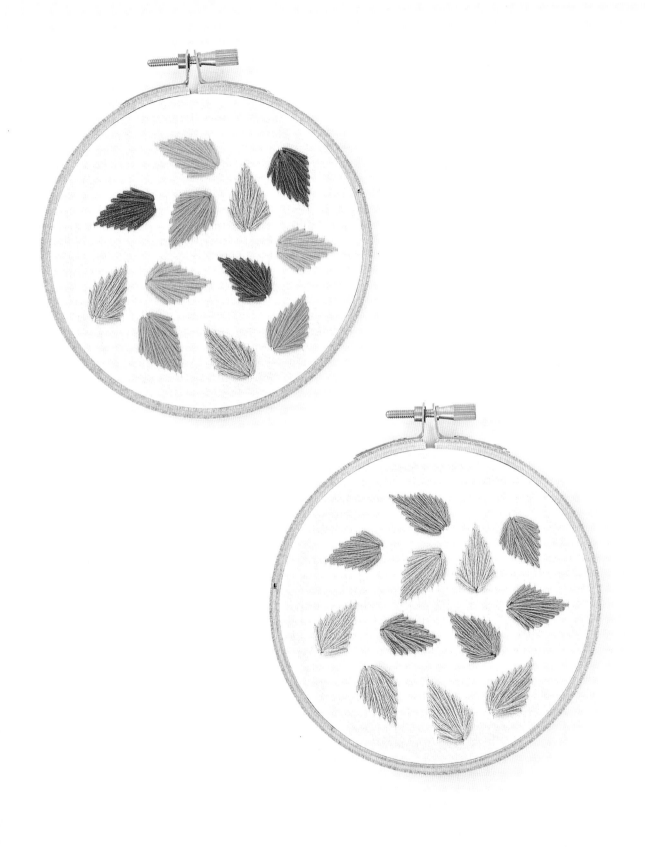

six

KNOTS

Knots are an unassumingly powerful skill to have in your embroidery arsenal. If you're brand new to embroidery, they are also likely to be your first big challenge. For such a tiny little element, they can be tricky. They're also beautiful and versatile. I utilize the texture and small size of them often as a filler, but they can be used from everything to dotting an "i" to creating the centers of flowers to being used together to create a lovely typography piece full of texture and interest.

FRENCH KNOT

Full disclosure: it took me forever to get the hang of the French knot! It's the back stitch of the knot family but not always so quick and easy to pick up. I've broken it down to every little detail and step so hopefully you won't have the same frustrations I had while learning.

The French knot will take both hands working together and some practice, but it's worth it, so take your time while learning. The texture is to die for.

In the patterns there will often be a dot or small circle where your French knot should be.

1. Bring your threaded needle up and through point A.

2. In your left hand, hold your thread as shown in the photo. In your right hand, hold your needle pointing toward your left hand.

3. For this step, your needle hand should remain stationary. Moving only your left hand, wrap the thread around your needle once.

4. Still loosely holding the thread in your left hand, use your right hand to push your needle halfway through your fabric at point B. Point B will be very close to point A. Gently pull on your thread with your left hand. This should bring your thread to the end of your needle and begin to form your knot.

5. Hold the thread under your left thumb, and use your right hand to begin to slowly pull your needle down through your fabric. Once the eye of the needle is through, you should see the knot clearly formed. Let go with your left thumb and pull the thread all the way through.

VARIATION: By wrapping the thread around your needle twice instead of once, you'll produce a larger knot as shown in photo 6 with the single wrap on the left and the double on the right.

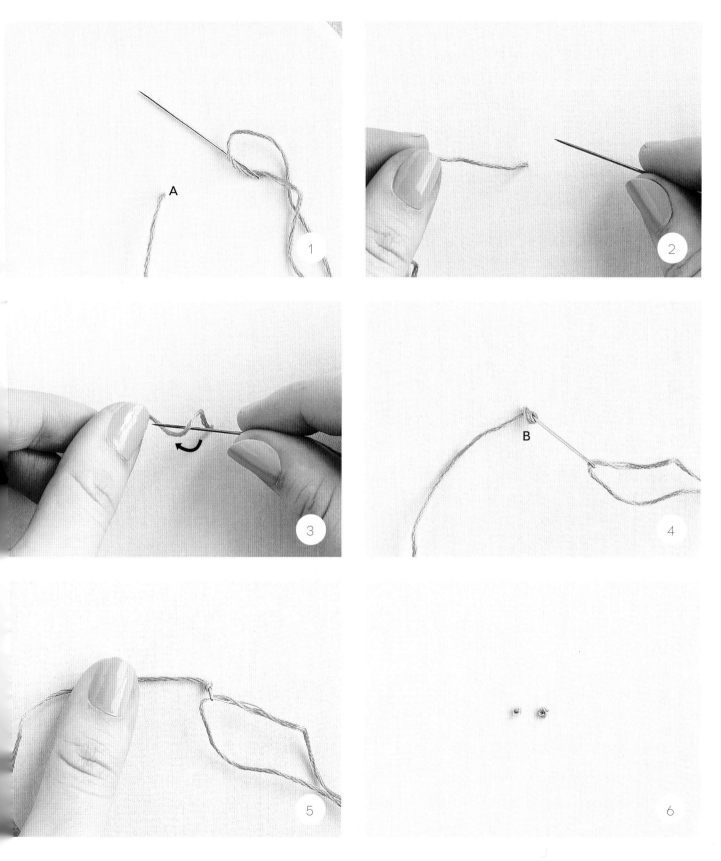

CONFETTI AMPERSAND

This confetti ampersand is a love letter to pretty typography and invaluable practice for French knots. It's also screaming for some customization. The possibilities here for any letter, shape or color palette are endless, and the texture in the finished project is to die for. I encourage you to try it not only to master the knot but to slow down and enjoy making them (because you're about to make a lot).

PATTERN USED: page 137

STITCHES USED: French knot (page 56)

HOOP SIZE: 4″ (10-cm) round

FABRIC COLOR SHOWN: Cream

COLOR PALETTE

CONFETTI: Light blue, medium blue, light yellow, peach, pink, light purple, pastel purple

Transfer the pattern to the fabric.

While this is very freeform, the trick to filling in shapes without them looking like blobs is to first start with the outline and work your way in. Make your first knots following the lines of the ampersand, then fill it in. I like to start with the first color, peppering the knots around with no real pattern; come in with the second color, etc. until you're at the end of your color list. Begin again with the first color, filling in any gaps until you're happy with how it looks.

COLONIAL KNOT

I mastered the colonial knot first, so I have an affinity for it. The colonial knot is a little bit larger than the French knot, and when you see it up close, it has an almost figure 8 shape to it.

I chose to include the colonial knot and the French knot because stitchers often find that they have a preference. They're both beautiful knots, so try them out and see which you like best.

If you've already mastered the French knot, a lot of this will be very similar in that you'll use both hands. The only real difference is the motion of the thread when it's wound around the needle.

1. Bring your threaded needle up through point A.

2. Holding your thread in your left hand, create a loop and place your needle into it.

3. Holding your right hand with the needle still, use your left hand to bring your thread over the needle in the opposite direction, then under again toward you. You should have a figure 8 shape on your needle.

4. Still loosely holding the thread in your left hand, use your right to place the needle halfway through the fabric at point B, very close to point A. Use your left hand to gently pull on your thread. This should pull the knot to the end of the needle.

5. Use your left thumb to gently hold the thread down. Use your right hand and begin to slowly pull your needle down through your fabric. Once the eye of the needle is through, you should see the knot begin to form. Let go with your left thumb and pull the thread all the way through.

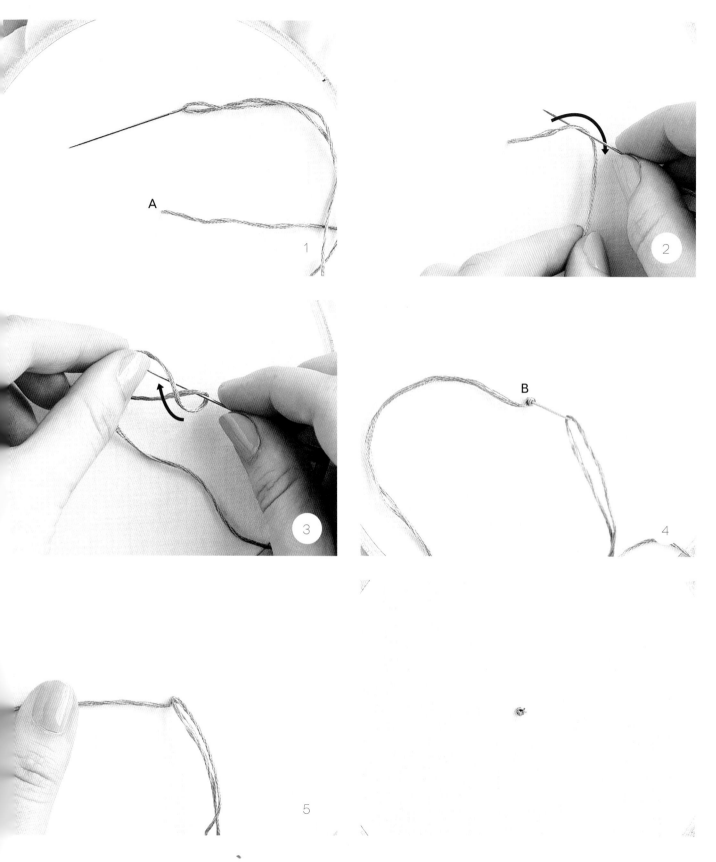

A

B

1

2

3

4

5

HANDFUL OF HYACINTHS

This design was inspired by vintage Victorian cards but with a modern twist. I wanted to evoke some of the elements of delicate strength in the simple line-work design of the disembodied hand while giving it something beautiful and floral to hold.

PATTERN USED: page 139

STITCHES USED: Back stitch (page 14), colonial knot (page 60), stem stitch (page 36), fern stitch (page 48)

HOOP SIZE: 7" (18-cm) round

FABRIC COLOR SHOWN: Cream

COLOR PALETTE
HAND & DECORATIVE SLEEVE CUFF:
Black

HYACINTHS: Dusty dark purple, medium purple, light dusty purple

STEMS: Medium olive green

LONG LEAVES: Olive green

FERN LEAVES: Medium blue green

Transfer the pattern to the fabric.

This is a very delicate style and pattern, so I encourage you to take your time with it. Begin first by back stitching the hand and sleeve cuff, using only three strands of floss. When you get to the small curves and details in the cuff, your stitches should be quite short so they don't look boxy or sharp.

Next, using colonial knots, start on your hyacinths, working from base to tip. I've used three shades of floss for a gradient look, but you can make them any color or colors you'd like. Once you're happy with your hyacinths, move on to the stems of your flowers using stem stitch. Fill in the rest of your pattern using back stitch for the long straight leaves and fern stitch for your ferns.

FLOWERS

Flowers and embroidery go together like peanut butter and jelly. It is a pairing as old as time, which is why I adore it so much. I love taking a classic and putting a modern twist on it. Much like the real thing, a lot of flower stitches, especially the ones I use and will be teaching, will grow and take shape organically. There are fewer rules and a lot more room for creativity as you grow your flowers petal by petal.

Learning the elements of floral embroidery will really elevate your work. They are versatile and will take any design to the next level (and impress your friends!). Some stitches, like the rose, may seem complicated, but they only look intimidating. I'll be breaking everything down step by step and sharing all of my secrets, tips and tricks that I've learned over the years to make it super easy.

STRAIGHT STITCH FLOWER

Straight stitch flowers are so simple and so lovely. I adore them. They're quick, easy, and adaptable. They can be sparse or full, perfectly round or a little wonky, and you can even use more than one color to give your flower dimension. We'll be using the stab technique to make them, which means pulling your needle and thread all the way through with each step.

These are easy to stitch without a pattern, but I like to draw a circle with a dot in the center as a guide when I work, and that's how they'll appear in this book as well. The outside of the circle is your guide for where your stitches should begin, working outward in. The dot in the center is your guide for where to stop. You should not stitch all the way to the center dot but just shy of it. There should be a small amount of space in the center for a knot stitch.

1. Bring your threaded needle up through point A and down through point B, which is just shy of our center dot.

2. Continue this motion, stitching outward in at point C to D, E to F and G to H. This will form the basis of our flower.

3. Working clockwise, begin to stitch a petal between your existing four stitches.

4. Repeat this process again, stitching between each existing petal. If you find any sparse sections after this, go back and fill them in as necessary. With a new threaded needle, come in through the center of your flower to create your knot of choice. In the example photo, I've chosen a single French knot.

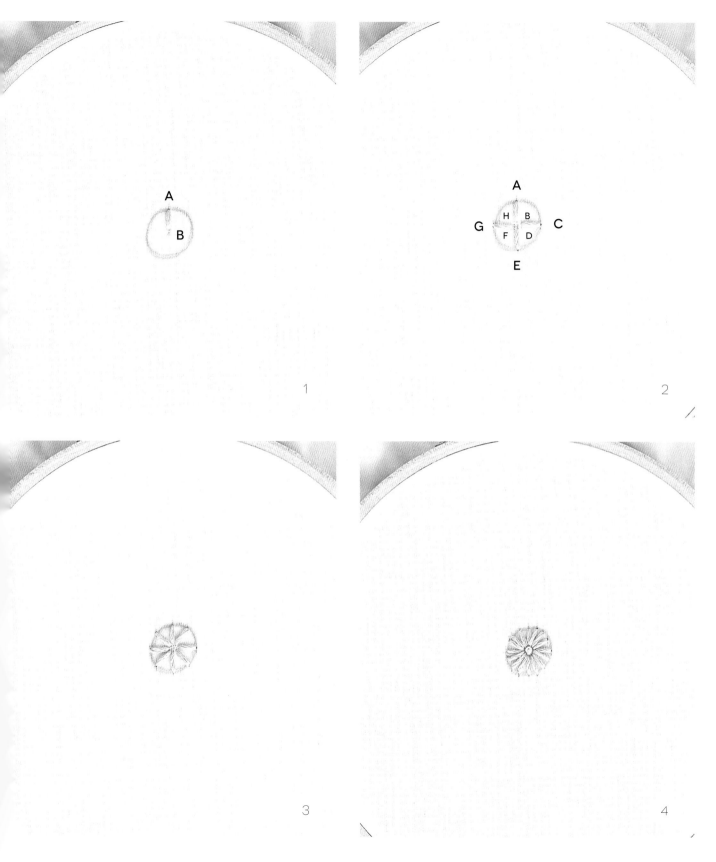

1

2

3

4

DON'T CARE FLORAL BORDER

This pattern makes excellent use of the straight stitch flower technique and is a great introductory example of how freeform you can be with floral design. I encourage you to add your own custom colors and sassy text!

PATTERN USED: page 141

STITCHES USED: Straight stitch flower (page 64), fern stitch (page 48), French knot (page 56), back stitch (page 14)

HOOP SIZE: 5" (13-cm) round

FABRIC COLOR SHOWN: Blue

COLOR PALETTE
FLOWERS: Light gray, light purple blue, light purple, gray purple

CENTER OF FLOWERS: Light yellow

FERN: Green

TEXT: Dark blue

Transfer the pattern to the fabric.

When I stitch up pieces with floral and text, I like to leave the text for last. Use all 6 strands of floss for all floral border elements and begin with the straight stitch flowers. To connect the flowers and create the border, use the fern stitch, working in the same counterclockwise direction. Fill in the centers of your flowers with your knot of choice.

For the text, use three strands of floss and back stitch for nice clean lines.

FLORAL BIRD SKULL

This delicate little bird skull is nestled gently among a bed of flowers. It's a reminder of how beautiful and tough nature can be, as I can imagine coming across a similar scene on a walk deep into the woods.

PATTERN USED: page 143

STITCHES USED: Back stitch (page 14), straight stitch flower (page 64), French knot (page 56), leaves (page 52), fern stitch (page 48)

HOOP SIZE: 5" (13-cm) round

FABRIC COLOR SHOWN: Cream

COLOR PALETTE

SKULL: Black

FLOWERS: Dusty light purple, gray, dusty medium red

CENTER OF FLOWERS: Medium yellow

LEAVES: Green

FERN: Medium green

KNOTS: Medium purple

Transfer the pattern to the fabric.

Begin first with the bird skull outline, using three strands of the black floss. Use long parallel back stitches to shade in its eyes and other details as shown in the finished photo.

Next, stitch up all of your straight stitch flowers using all six strands of floss. Fill in the centers using a French or colonial knot with all six strands of the yellow floss. Once you're happy with your flowers, stitch up your leaves, then come in with the fern stitch. To finish up the floral work, come in with the medium purple floss to fill in any little gaps using the French knot.

LAZY DAISY

Ready for a challenge? If you're new to embroidery or haven't tried the lazy daisy stitch, it's probably going to feel a little weird at first. To complete a single petal will take a few steps, but before you know it, you'll be stitching fields of daisies in no time.

What you need to pay attention to the most here is the tension you use to pull on your thread when you create the loop that will become your petal. This stitch also requires the use of both hands working together. While most used for flowers, their teardrop shape makes perfect leaves when used individually.

The pattern shown in the example is of the final shape of our daisy. Don't be concerned if yours doesn't match up perfectly. The lazy daisy often has a mind of its own, so think of it more as a guide for size and shape. As with the straight stitch flower, make sure to leave a small amount of room in the center so it can be filled with a knot to finish.

1. The first step is to create a loop with your thread that will become your petal. Bring your threaded needle up through A and down through B but not all the way through. A and B should be very close together but not touching. Leave a length of floss at least twice as long as the petal shown in the pattern. Lay your loop upward and flat.

2. Bring your needle up through C, with your loop surrounding it, and begin to gently pull your thread through straight upward. Your petal should be starting to take form.

3. Pulling too hard will create thin and sharp petals. Keeping it too loose can look sloppy. Take your time to find a happy medium. Once you're happy with the shape, bring your needle down through D. The point here is to secure your petal between C and D. They should be close together on each side of your loop.

4. Repeat this process working clockwise around your flower pattern, remembering to leave a little bit of space in the center.

5. Once your petals are complete, bring a new threaded needle up from the center of your flower and create a knot of your choice.

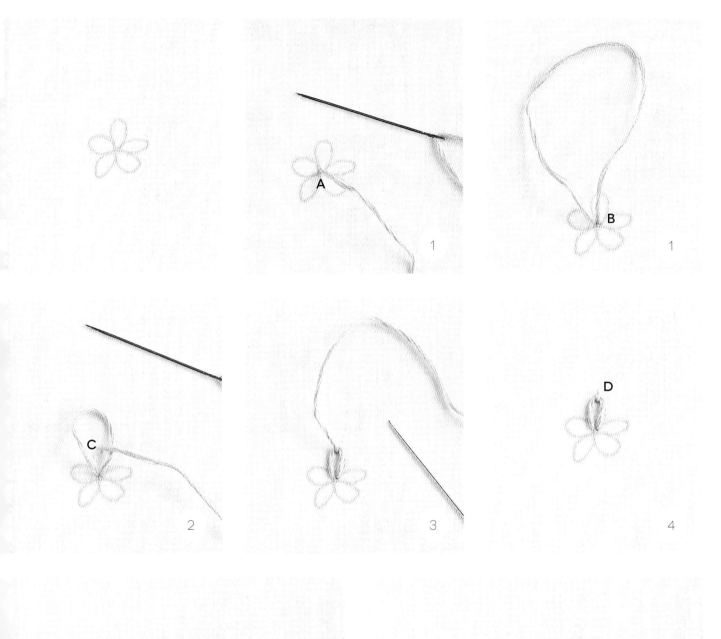

HELL YES DAISY CHAIN

This sweet little daisy chain is bursting with some positive vibes. Is it also perfect for adding your own sassy text? Hell yes!

PATTERN USED: page 145

STITCHES USED: Lazy daisy (page 70), back stitch (page 14), French knot (page 56)

HOOP SIZE: 6" (15-cm) round

FABRIC COLOR SHOWN: Blue

COLOR PALETTE

DAISIES: White

CENTER OF DAISIES: Light yellow

VINE: Green

TEXT: Black

Transfer the pattern to the fabric.

This is a very simple, straightforward design as well as fantastic practice for the lazy daisy stitch. Begin with your daisies, using the lazy daisy stitch. Use the back stitch next for your vines. Once that's completed, go back in and fill in the centers of your flowers with the knot of your choice.

For the text, use three strands of floss and back stitch for nice clean lines.

SATIN STITCH FLOWER

If you haven't learned the basics of satin stitch or leaves, that would be a great place to start as this is very similar, but it isn't necessary. We'll be using a lot of the same techniques to create a beautiful and full flower. These flowers are fantastic on their own or as part of a floral embroidery pattern.

I like to work petal by petal, starting in the middle of each and working my way out for a clean look. The pattern shows each petal with a circle in the center, which we'll be saving for last.

1. Choose your starting petal and bring your needle up and through point A, then down and through point B. This should be even in the center of your first petal.

2. Begin stitching down the left side of your petal, C to D. Your stitches should be close together so no gaps of fabric are showing, but wider at the top and tapering down to create the soft, round petal shape. Continue this same motion down each side of your flower. If you notice any bare spots, go back and fill them in.

3. Repeat these steps, working your way around your petal, remembering to leave the center empty.

4. With your petals completed, it's time to fill in the center. In the example, I used satin stitch to create the circle. Alternately, you can fill the center with a grouping of knots for more texture.

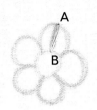

1

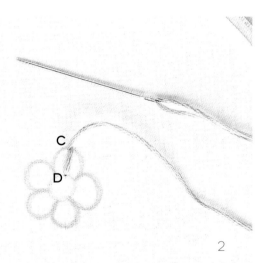

2

2

3

4

FLORAL SHARK ATTACK

This shark got a little surprise when he jumped out of the water into a bunch of flowers.
A little sharp, a little sweet. This pattern has a bite to it.

PATTERN USED: page 147

STITCHES USED: Back stitch (page 14),
satin stitch flower (page 74), leaves
(page 52)

HOOP SIZE: 7" (18-cm) round

FABRIC COLOR SHOWN: Blue

COLOR PALETTE

SHARK: Black

CENTER FLOWER: Dusty light purple

SIDE FLOWERS: Dusty peach,
dusty pink

FLOWER CENTERS: Light yellow

LEAVES: Medium green, light green

Transfer the pattern to the fabric.

Begin with the shark. Using all six strands of your black floss, use back stitch for
the body. When you get to the teeth, use single long back stitches so the lines are
clean and sharp.

Using all six strands of floss, use what you've learned with satin stitch flower to
create the flowers. Once those are completed, stitch up the leaves. As shown in the
finished photo, I've used two shades of green for some depth.

MOONRISE ROSES

The most common question I get asked is, "How do you do those roses?" Over the years I've perfected my own technique because I never found one that I liked. Either they were too boxy or too loose or looked too perfect or unnatural.

So, finally, I'm teaching you how I do "those roses," which I've named the Moonrise Rose, after my business.

There are three steps to these roses and each has a very important purpose. I'll be breaking down and explaining each step so it's as clear and simple as it can be while you learn. The knot will likely be the most difficult part, but it doesn't have to be perfect. Chances are it will be slightly covered by your base stitches, so don't stress it too much.

The pattern I use for roses is a circle with a small square in the center. The square acts as a guide for your knot, while the outside circle is a guide for the size of the finished rose.

STEP ONE: The base of the Moonrise Rose is a flat square knot. I love the overall effect of it even though it's a small part overall. It's a large and sturdy knot that holds up well to all of the petals that will be built around it. Alternately, you could use a group of French or colonial knots as the center base of your rose.

1. Using the square as your guide, come up and through point A, then down and through point B.

2. Bring your needle up and through point C. Keeping your thread to the right of your needle, slide it under your first stitch (A to B). Do not pierce your fabric. Gently pull your needle up and to the left until the thread is taut.

3. Keeping your thread to the left of your needle, slide it under your first stitch (A to B) again, but don't pull it through yet.

4. Moving your thread from left to right, tuck it under your needle as shown. Gently pull your needle up until the thread is taut. You should see the knot form. Be careful to not pull too tightly or you could distort the knot.

5. To finish, pierce your needle down into point D and pull all the way through. Your knot should look as it does in the example photo. Do not finish this with a knot at the back, as we're jumping right into step two.

(continued)

1

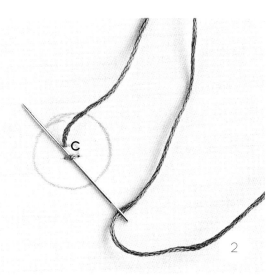

2

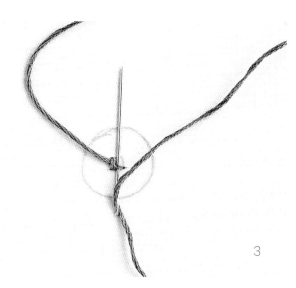

3

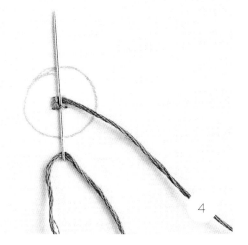

4

5

STEP TWO: The second step is the base of the rose, which will compose most of it. We'll be working clockwise with overlapping single stitches around the center knot to slowly form petals. Gradually lengthen your stitches as your rose gets larger. The goal here is to keep the rose as round and soft as you can, but it doesn't have to be perfect. The last step will polish any mistakes.

6. Using the same threaded needle, begin to build your petals by using short diagonal single stitches around your knot in the same clockwise direction.

7. As you work around your rose, your stitches should naturally and gradually begin to become longer as your rose gets larger. Even-length stitches aren't important here. Keep stitching around your knot until you are almost at the size of your rose outline. Your rose should look similar to the one in the example photo at this point. It's great as is, but the final step is what takes it to the next level and makes it a Moonrise Rose.

FINAL STEP: To create a beautiful, soft and organic-looking rose with larger petals, the last few stitches are different from those in step two. We're still using the same thread but will start to work in the opposite direction, with our stitches now longer and "tucked" under. This will feel very similar to the stem stitch.

8. Beginning now counterclockwise, bring your needle up through point A and down through point B. This first stitch will be longer than any of your other stitches, and point B will be tucked under your previous stitches. Continue around your rose in the same direction.

9. As your rose gets larger and your stitches become longer, use your thumb to gently hold your thread to the outside as you pull your needle down and through. This helps to keep your stitch from slipping over your rose. Your final stitches should be fairly loose to create a soft look.

10. Ideally, you want at least two rows of these petals around your finished flower by the time it's to the desired size. If any spots looks pointy or lopsided, go back and add petals as needed.

No two Moonrise Roses will ever be alike. Each step and technique serves a purpose in creating the perfect rose, but it's not an exact science. Take your time and let them form organically.

6

7

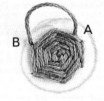

8

8

9

10

FINGERS CROSSED

This design was inspired by a modern take on line-work drawings. I like to think that you could attribute your own meaning to the crossed fingers. It's often seen as a symbol of wishing for luck, but it can also be a bit mischievous, as you might cross your fingers behind your back when telling a lie.

PATTERN USED: page 149

STITCHES USED: Back stitch (page 14), Moonrise Rose (page 78), satin stitch flower (page 74), straight stitch flower (page 64), leaves (page 52), French knot (page 56)

HOOP SIZE: 7" (18-cm) round

FABRIC COLOR SHOWN: Cream

COLOR PALETTE
HAND: Black

ROSE: Terra cotta red

SATIN STITCH FLOWER: Dusty purple

LARGE STRAIGHT STITCH FLOWERS: Dusty medium pink

SMALL STRAIGHT STITCH FLOWERS: Light blue

FLOWER CENTERS: Light yellow

LEAVES: Medium green, dark green

FILLER: Light purple

Transfer the pattern to the fabric.

Of the Moonrise Rose projects, this will likely be the easiest when it comes to the florals. Begin first with the hand, using only three strands of floss and using back stitch.

For the florals, use all 6 strands of thread for each element. Begin with the center rose, using the Moonrise Rose stitch. Next, finish the satin stitch and straight stitch flowers on the sides. Using a French knot, add the flower centers. Once you're happy with your flowers, come in with the leaves stitch, alternating between the two shades of green for more depth. Finally, use French knots to fill in around the flowers.

GOOD LUCK

This piece was inspired by a Victorian-era greeting card. I love working with juxtaposition and was struck by the mix of a heavy metal horseshoe and its symbolism of luck and good fortune surrounded by lovely draping floral work.

PATTERN USED: page 151

STITCHES USED: Back stitch (page 14), Moonrise Rose (page 78), satin stitch flower (page 74), straight stitch flower (page 64), leaves (page 52), fern stitch (page 48), French knot (page 56)

HOOP SIZE: 7" (18-cm) round

FABRIC COLOR SHOWN: Cream

COLOR PALETTE

HORSESHOE: Gold

TEXT: Deep dusty purple

ROSES: Terra cotta

SATIN STITCH FLOWER: Medium pink purple

STRAIGHT STITCH FLOWER: Medium blue

FLOWER CENTERS: Yellow

LEAVES: Medium and light green

FERN: Light olive green

KNOTS: Dusty purple

Transfer the pattern to the fabric.

I'd definitely place this pattern in the advanced category, but I don't want that to intimidate you. It only looks complicated. Break it down piece by piece, and it'll come together easily.

Start with the horseshoe, using back stitch and all six strands of floss. Save the text for last.

For the florals spilling around the horseshoe, begin with the one large and one small rose using the moonrise rose stitch and all six strands of floss. Next, stitch the large satin stitch flower and the two petals peeking out from behind the horseshoe. Lastly, complete the straight stitch flowers. Take a step back and look at your flowers and go back and fill in any gaps if necessary.

Go in with your leaves to bring the floral design together, alternating the two shades of green for more depth, then move on to the ferns. Finish up the florals by filling in the centers of your straight stitch flowers with your knot of choice. Go back with French or colonial knots throughout the design to add texture and help fill any small gaps.

Lastly, use back stitch and three strands of floss to stitch up your text. This is also a great design to incorporate your own custom text in.

FLORAL CROWN COW SKULL

Just like the trophies on an old hunter's wall, this stoic cow skull makes a beautiful
addition to your wall. Bonus: You don't have to have an actual dead animal in your house.
The flower crown adds a modern touch to this classic wall hanging.

PATTERN USED: page 153

STITCHES USED: Back stitch (page 14),
satin stitch (page 26), Moonrise Rose
(page 78), leaves (page 52), fern stitch
(page 48)

HOOP SIZE: 8" (20-cm) round

FABRIC COLOR SHOWN: Cream

COLOR PALETTE

SKULL: Black

ROSES: Medium dusty pink, light dusty
pink, medium terra cotta

LEAVES: Medium blue green

FERN AND SHORT STEMS: Olive green

SMALL FLOWERS: Light blue

KNOTS: Gold yellow

Transfer the pattern to the fabric.

This floral pattern has a lot of room for extra bits of creativity, so I encourage you
to add floral elements as you'd like.

Start by back stitching the skull and horns using three strands of floss. When you
get to the eyes and the nose, use satin stitch techniques to fill them in, still using
the three strands of floss. When you're happy with your cow skull, move on to the
floral elements. Always start with the largest objects, which in this case are the
Moonrise Roses. Next, stitch the leaves using six strands of floss. When you get
to the fern stitches and small flower stems, use only three strands of floss so they
have a more delicate look. Use six strands of floss for your small flowers.

Take a step back and look at your flower crown. If you want a fuller look, go back
and add any greenery or flowers as you see fit. Knots also make a great floral filler.

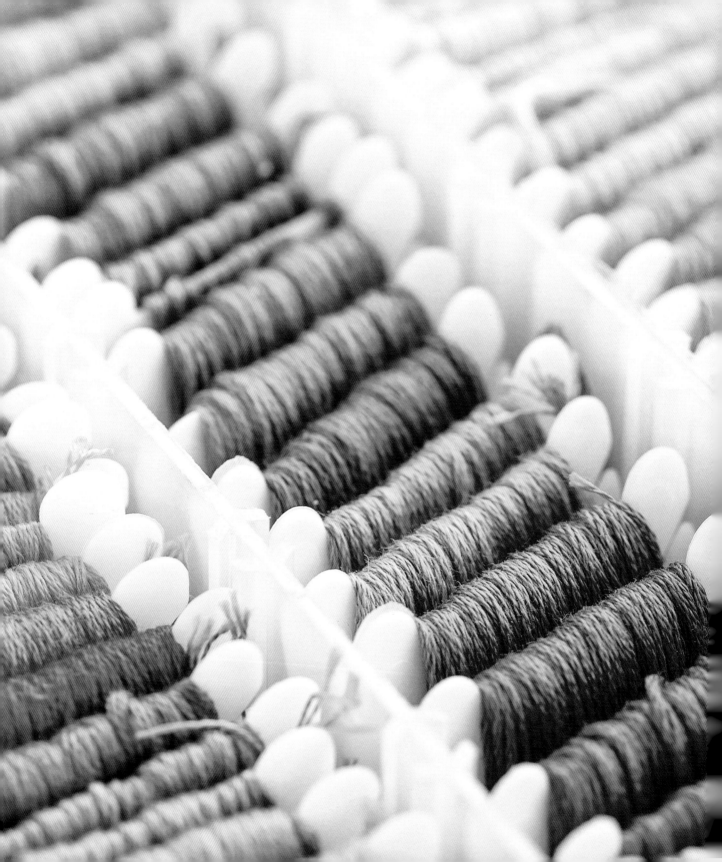

eight

TOOLS OF THE TRADE

You don't necessarily need anything special to begin embroidery. When it comes to needles and floss, however, I don't mess around. For being such small items, they make a world of difference. The good news is that they're available at any decent craft store and inexpensive. Trust me, I've wasted a lot of time in the past messing with crappy needles and floss. It's not worth it. Treat yourself to the best.

NEEDLES

Using the proper needle is imperative. It should feel comfortable in your fingers, easily pierce through the fabric, and have an eye large enough for your embroidery floss. Sewing needles do not work here. Oftentimes they are too thin and too short, and the eye is too small to accommodate embroidery floss.

Embroidery needles are easy to find. They're usually next to the embroidery floss and conveniently labeled "embroidery needles."

They come in a variety of lengths and sizes. While I personally prefer to work with a size 5 embroidery needle, I encourage you to try out different sizes and lengths to find what works best for your hands. Most craft stores carry a variety pack of needles for this.

FLOSS

FLOSS VERSUS THREAD

You've probably seen the terms floss and thread used interchangeably. I usually refer to floss as thread out of habit, but there is a distinct difference between the two. What we'll be using is actually floss, not thread, so I've been referring to it as such throughout the book.

First and foremost, whichever type you choose to use, make sure it's high-quality floss. It changes everything. Low-quality floss is more difficult to work with, and your finished project will not have that clean, polished look. You may find that some fibers are coarse and can even break off or shred. Not a good look.

EMBROIDERY FLOSS

Simple and to the point, this is the most commonly used floss. Because it is so popular and widely available, the color selection is amazing. It is made from six individual mercerized cotton strands gently twisted together. When you purchase a high-quality brand, it will be easy to work with and have a beautiful sheen to it.

Brand availability may differ depending on where you live, but I personally prefer and use DMC brand throughout this book.

As tempting as they may be—especially for a beginner—I do not recommend the bargain bulk bags of embroidery floss. They're often poor quality.

PEARL/PERLE COTTON FLOSS

The main difference between pearl or perle cotton floss and regular embroidery floss is that pearl/perle cotton floss comes in a variety of thicknesses and does not separate. It's made of twisted high-mercerized cotton, which makes it extra shiny. If you choose to use this style of floss, keep in mind that the texture of it will change the look of the stitches.

METALLIC EMBROIDERY FLOSS

While beautiful, metallic embroidery floss is notoriously difficult to work with. Because of the synthetic fibers, the threads are not soft and they tangle easily. I've found that they work best for accents or pops of color and are easier to work with when separated into fewer strands than the standard six.

SCISSORS

While you certainly don't need any fancy scissors to begin embroidery, there are a lot of great tools available that will make your life easier when it comes to cutting fabric and thread.

Here are a few of the popular options.

CLASSIC STORK SCISSORS

Yup, just like Grandma's. She was on to something, though. Not only are they beautiful, but that long beak is perfect for getting into small spaces like taking out stitches and cutting thread. Because of their small size, however, they're not ideal for cutting fabric.

SNIPPERS

Snippers are my personal favorite. Not only do they look badass, but they're sharp as hell. Because of the simple design and long handle, they're easy to grab and snip thread quickly as you work. They're a great utility scissor, but they're not ideal for larger items because of their short blades.

SEAM RIPPER

If you've ever sewn, you know how great a classic seam ripper tool is to have on hand when you need to take out a lot of stitches. It's also a great substitute if you don't have any scissors with a small, sharp point—you can get into tight spaces without accidentally cutting your fabric or the wrong thread.

SEWING SCISSORS

There are a lot of definitions, sizes and styles of sewing scissors. Generally, they're a larger pair of scissors that are comfortable on the hands, with extra-sharp blades that cut through fabric with ease.

There are tons of scissors out there, but these are the basics. Whichever you choose, I recommend one pair that cuts fabric well and one pair with a small, sharp point to get into tiny spaces.

PATTERN TRANSFER TOOLS

An essential tool in embroidery is what you choose to mark your pattern onto your fabric. Depending on the fabric and personal preference, there are a lot of items to choose from. Below are some of the most common:

WATER SOLUBLE FABRIC PEN OR MARKER

This is my preferred tool for pattern transfer and what I use every day. I like to use the fine point pen option, but you may also find markers at your local craft store, usually near sewing supplies. They're made specifically for fabric and mark cleanly and easily. When you're finished with your project, simply rinse it under water and the ink disappears completely. You don't have to worry about lines showing on your final project. I tend to add or change things as I work, so these pens are perfect for scribblers like me.

PENCIL

A regular graphite pencil is another popular option. Since it's not necessarily made for this task, be careful when transferring your pattern and stitching so you don't have any pencil lines showing in your final project.

PENS OR MARKER

Similar to regular pencils, these will do the trick but aren't made for this, so you'll have some extra steps and cautions along the way. While I recommend washing your final project, you may want to skip that step if you used a regular pen or marker to transfer your pattern onto your fabric as it will likely bleed and ruin the final design.

WHITE FABRIC PENCIL

These pencils are a great tool to have on hand when working with darker fabrics where regular marking tools won't show up. You can remove excess pencil markings on your finished project with a damp cloth. You can find these at your local craft store, often in the sewing section.

nine

MATERIALS

HOOPS

Embroidery hoops are one of my most favorite things in the world. You should see the way my eyes light up when my bulk hoop order arrives or I find a beautiful vintage hoop at the thrift store. Straight-up actual heart eyes.

Seriously, though. They're essential to hand embroidery, so let's talk embroidery hoops!

The most common embroidery hoops you'll find today are made from wood with a metal screw closure at the top. They're widely available, affordable, versatile and durable. Sizes typically range from as small as 3 inches (8 cm) to a humongous 14 inches (36 cm) and beyond. I prefer to stitch in them even if my project will be set in a different style of hoop, because they're comfortable in the hands and provide good tension.

Embroidery hoops are made from two separate rings. The inner ring is a plain circle and the slightly larger outer ring sports an adjustable metal closure at the top. This is used to adjust the tension so your fabric can be stretched securely between the rings while you work and set your finished project to be displayed.

When you're purchasing embroidery hoops at a store make sure to take a minute and check each one out. Not all are made equal. Make sure the screw at the top is working and doesn't stick. Also check that the inner and outer ring fit well together, with no large gaps. Nothing makes embroidery more frustrating than a hoop that doesn't want to cooperate.

PLASTIC

Your local craft store may also carry some plastic hoops along with the common wood ones, usually in an array of colors. Depending on the brand and style, you may find that you like to stitch in them rather than using wood hoops. They're also great decorative hoops for finished pieces but tend to be more costly.

VINTAGE

Finding a beautiful vintage embroidery hoop is like striking gold for me. Oftentimes they are fragile, so I prefer to stitch in a wood hoop, then transfer the embroidered fabric to the vintage hoop to be set for display.

Here are a few kinds you may run into at thrift or vintage shops.

PLASTIC FAUX WOOD GRAIN

While these hoops are plastic, they have a textured wood look and color to them. The inner ring is hard plastic while the outside is a bendable, softer plastic made to stretch around the inner ring. It has a decorative metal loop at the top for hanging. This style is still made today, though depending on what country you live in, brand-new ones may not be readily available in stores or online.

METAL

Metal embroidery hoops are fantastic finds. You may find one that is shiny and clean or heavily marked with patina. The inner ring is lined with cork where it meets the outer ring. The outer ring has a metal spring closure at the top so it has a small amount of stretch to it.

WOOD

There are myriad vintage wood styles, and I've found that they're the most durable versus plastic and metal as they're less likely to degrade, tarnish or bend.

FABRIC

The second most common question I get asked, after "How do you do those roses?" (see page 78), is about what fabric I use. There seems to be this idea that there are "right" and "wrong" fabrics and that the correct answers are closely guarded secrets in the embroidery world.

The truth is that it's all really a matter of preference when you're armed with the knowledge of what works best and what doesn't. If a needle can go through it, you can embroider it. However, certain fabrics will produce beautiful results and be easy on your hands while others will make your life a living hell.

I'd never actually paid too much attention to the nitty-gritty details of fabrics (weave pattern, thread count, fibers, etc.) until a few years ago. I went largely by feel and intuition, with a lot of trial and error, to find what worked and what sucked. With embroidery being such a tactile medium, you, too, may have to try out a few fabrics before you find what you like. The good news is that I'll be sharing all of my embroidery fabric knowledge so you won't feel like a lost lamb in the fabric aisles like I did.

First up, to finally answer the question "What fabric do you use?": My go-to that I've used for years in my personal work and throughout this book is a cream-colored 100 percent cotton sateen fabric in a mid-high price range. It is a tighter weave but soft and easy to work with. It has a subtle sheen that pairs beautifully with my floss. I went through at least five other fabrics until I found this one and have been using it ever since. Otherwise, I tend to stick with 100 percent cotton fabric when choosing other colors or patterns. Cotton is durable, reliable, widely available and comes in an endless array of finishes.

Let's talk fabric basics. First and foremost, keep in mind what your fabric will be used for: embroidery. It will be mercilessly stabbed with a needle and filled with embroidery floss. Make sure it's up to the task. I've broken down what to look for and what to avoid so you can walk through the fabric aisles with confidence.

FIBERS

Natural fibers are always recommended. They're less likely to do anything weird on you or be tough on your floss. However, there are some synthetic fabrics and blends that may work well for you if they pass the embroidery tests below. When in doubt, try it out!

WEAVE/THREAD COUNT/FEEL

On their own, weave and thread count are quite technical, whereas feel is just that: How does it feel in your hands? I've grouped them together here because they go hand in hand. You don't need to be a textile expert. The point of these three criteria is how the needle and floss work together with your fabric.

Take a close look at your fabric. If the weave is too loose and you can see gaps, it may not be the best fit for your embroidery project, as it won't hold its own against your stitches. If the weave is too tight or feels stiff, you may have difficulty working your needle and thread through it, which will be hard on your hands and can lead to a puckered look with your stitches.

Using your eyes is important here, but getting a feel for the fabric with your hands can often tell you more than your sight alone. If you're unsure, go for a fabric that is soft to the touch.

QUALITY AND COST

Another very important factor is the quality of your fabric. With fabric, you get what you pay for. Always begin your search in the mid-high price range. After you peruse high-quality fabrics, you'll likely find that the lower quality may look and feel like straw in comparison. The good news is that embroidery doesn't use a lot of fabric, so you can purchase the amount you need without breaking the bank. Not only will your finished project that you worked so hard on look amazing, but your hands will thank you for not choosing crappy fabric that is hard to work with.

COLOR

The color of your fabric is almost as important as your stitches since it's your base. When in doubt, go with a mellow neutral. If you're not sure, take your thread colors with you to lay against the fabric to see if it works. Keep your pattern marker color in mind as well. Make sure you have a way to transfer your pattern onto your fabric so that you can actually see it. If your transfer marker is blue and so is your fabric, you're going to have some issues.

PATTERN

Similar to color, choosing the right patterned fabric is very important. It can also be difficult. If it's too busy, there's little to no chance that your design will show. If it's too colorful, some thread colors may be washed out. I recommend finding patterned fabric where both the base color and pattern color are mellow and similar in shade.

VINTAGE FABRIC

If you love vintage and secondhand stores like I do, you probably also covet beautiful vintage fabrics. Since chances are there will be zero information about what the fabric is made of or how old it is, you really have to use your intuition and what you've learned here. Some fabrics, due to their age and often mysterious origins, may be very difficult to stitch through. I often use these for small projects. They're great for short and simple text-only embroidery projects that don't kill your fingers and let the gorgeous vintage fabric shine.

STRETCH

How much stretch should your embroidery have? Ideally, none to very, very little. You want your stitches to hold up even when they're out of the hoop, so using a stretchy fabric is a bad idea because your stitches may warp or pucker. I've used fabrics with a little bit of stretch to them before, and while it's not impossible, it's not ideal. You have to be incredibly careful when setting your hoop so your design doesn't look wonky after all that hard work.

Okay, we've learned a lot about fabric. If you're sitting there thinking, "Just tell me what fabric to buy, already!" this is my answer: mid-high price range, 100 percent cotton, no stretch, soft to the touch.

Ten

ORGANIZATION

Confession time: I tend to be a little ridiculous when it comes to organizing my embroidery supplies. I find that my brain works best when I know exactly where every little thing is, and, let's be real, there's nothing more beautiful than a perfectly color-coordinated floss box full of wound bobbins.

My setup involves a vintage-style three-level cart. The bottom shelf is hoops, the middle is neatly folded fabrics organized by color and style, and the top holds my tools and thread boxes with my pattern and sketch binder. You don't have to be as meticulous about it as I am, but it's worth putting some thought into. Below are some tips and tools.

BOBBINS

Are you obsessed with floss yet? I am! With the amount of colors and styles available, it's easy to begin with a few skeins, then suddenly have a massive floss ball taking over your home. Do yourself a favor and start winding your skeins on bobbins from the beginning. I know this task can drive some people crazy, but slow down, take the time to do it, then thank me later.

You can find bobbins made specifically for this near the floss. They're perforated little squares of cardboard or plastic with a hole at the top. The cardboard bobbins are a great option for beginners, but the plastic are vastly more durable.

First, and this is very important, make sure to write the color number on your bobbin. There should be a space in the top corner. Most floss skeins are identified by number, not the name of the color, so don't forget this step.

Unwrap your skein of floss and gently grab the free end, usually at the bottom, and start winding around your bobbin. The trick to not creating a huge knot is to take your time. If done correctly, you should not create a single knot. If you do create a knot you aren't able to undo, simply cut the knot out and continue winding the rest of the floss on. There are notches in the bottom of the bobbin to secure the floss when you come to the end.

FLOSS BOX

Boxes are a great little investment to keep your bobbins in one place and grouped by color. Not only is everything neat and organized now, but you can see at a glance when you're running low on a color and exactly which number it is.

BOBBIN RING

I only recently started using a bobbin ring, and I've been wondering where it's been all my life. Usually found with the bobbins, it's a simple metal ring that opens at the top. They're made to hold your bobbins through the hole in the top center. When I'm about to start working on a new project, I pull my bobbins from my floss box and set them in my ring. Now you've got your colors handy in one spot! Easy-peasy.

BONUS: If you're like me, you have a hard time simply throwing away all of those beautiful colorful floss ends and bits. The best way to keep them is to start a collection jar! I've amassed enough floss over the years to fill up a few vintage jars, and they sit on my shelves as a decorative reminder of past projects. Plus, they're just so darn cute.

eleven

FINISHING UP

WASHING YOUR STITCHED FABRIC

Even if you haven't chosen to use a water-soluble fabric pen or marker, which requires this step, I suggest washing your finished piece before you set it, for a nice polished look.

First, place a clean towel on a flat, dry surface. Remove your fabric from the hoop and, holding it flat with both hands, place it under gently running cool water for about 10 to 15 seconds. Place it on your clean, dry towel, making sure there are no folds or wrinkles. Leave it to air dry. If you want to speed the process up a little bit, you can place it in the sun or near a fan.

This is really more of a gentle rinse than a wash. You don't need soap, and scrubbing could damage your piece. It's tempting to want to "dry" your piece with the towel, especially floral work, which uses a lot of thread and soaks up water, but resist that urge. If you try to squeeze water out or pat it dry, you may accidentally mess up your stitches.

If some of the stitches look loose or distorted while it dries, that's okay. If you've done it right, they'll be back to normal once it's stretched in the hoop.

SETTING YOUR HOOP

Once your project is finished, washed and dried, it's time to set it into the hoop. If you want to jazz up your hoop (see Hoop Treatments, page 100), now is the time to do it.

Setting your hoop refers to permanently securing the fabric to the back of the hoop with glue so it's ready to be displayed.

Next up, it's time to choose your glue.

HOT GLUE: Working with a hot glue gun is a little faster than regular glue because it sets within seconds. Keeping that in mind, work in smaller sections so it doesn't cool before you press the fabric to it. Also, be careful of burning your fingers, as there will only be a layer of fabric between the hot glue and your hands.

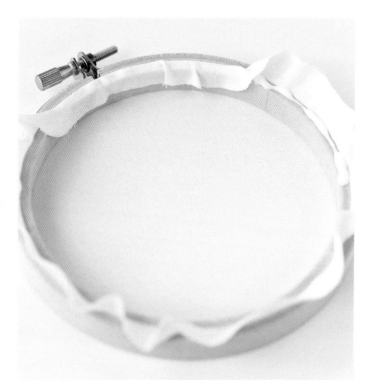

WOOD SAFE GLUE: Regular glue takes some more time to work with and set, but you don't have to mess with glue guns or risk burned fingers. When using regular glue, you may have to double back and press the fabric down again, as some pieces can become unstuck. Also, make sure to give it ample drying time, at least an hour.

First, stretch your fabric into the hoop. Now is the time to be picky. Make sure it's even, straight and centered. If you're not sure, hang it up on the wall and take a step back to look at it. Once you start cutting and gluing, there's no going back.

When you're happy with the placement, turn it over to the backside. Using a sharp pair of scissors, trim the excess fabric, following the line of the hoop so you have approximately half an inch (1.3 cm) left. This fabric will be glued to the inner ring. It should be long enough to wrap around the edge but not long enough to touch your stretched fabric in front. Trim accordingly.

Start with a short line of glue on the rim of your inner embroidery ring. Press your fabric to it, wrapping it gently on the inside. This may take some practice at first. You want enough glue to secure your fabric but not enough that it spills out or runs into your stretched fabric in front. Continue this around your hoop, going back if any sections need more glue or come unstuck. Once you're finished, lay it facedown on a clean flat surface to dry.

Don't be too frustrated if your fabric is being tricky. More glue and patience usually does the trick. It doesn't have to be perfect, but you want it to lie flat against the rim of your hoop so it will lie flat against a wall if you choose to hang it.

Once your hoop is dry, it's ready to display! There are many ways to hang up an embroidery hoop. The easiest and most common is to place a thumbtack or nail in your wall and hang it by the adjustable closure, or simply place the hoop against the wall, situating the nail under the lip of the inner ring. You can also tie a loop of ribbon or string around the adjustable closure to hang it by.

HOOP TREATMENTS

A plain wood embroidery hoop is great on its own but is also the perfect blank canvas. There are a lot of ways to spruce your hoops up or match them to your designs or home decor. While you certainly could, I don't recommend stitching in treated hoops. This is best done after your embroidery is completed and ready to be set. Here are some common treatments.

STAINING

If you've never stained wood before, you'll be surprised how quick and easy it is. All you need is a small can of wood stain, some gloves and some scrap cloth. Make sure to follow the instructions on the stain you purchase, but the basic process involves dipping your cloth in the stain and rubbing it into your wood hoop. Stain only the outer ring on the outside and sides. There's no reason to stain the inside that lies against the fabric as it won't be visible in the finished product.

Use a paper towel to remove any excess stain if necessary, and let your stained hoop dry for at least eight hours.

PAINTING

Wood hoops are also great canvasses for paint. Those inexpensive little acrylic craft paints are perfect for this. They're available in a wide variety of colors and finishes, including matte, glossy, metallic and glittery. Using a brush or sponge, paint your hoops to your heart's desire. Let them dry for at least two hours before you set your embroidered fabric in them.

RIBBON

If you want to add some softness to your hoop, wrapping ribbon around it is a nice option. Like all treatments, this is only done to the outside ring. Measure out a length of ribbon that is at least four times as long as the circumference of your hoop. Using a wood-safe glue, first secure your ribbon to the hoop at the top by wrapping it around twice. Slowly work your way around the hoop by wrapping it as evenly as you can, using an occasional spot of glue to secure it. Cut off any excess ribbon and glue the end down on the inside of the hoop where you won't see it. Let dry for at least an hour.

STAMPS

Most wood hoops take to ink well, and you can stamp on them as you would paper. Depending on the wood, you may find some ink will bleed. If you're not sure, test the ink on your inner ring, since it's not seen once your project is finished.

DIY PATTERN MAKING

When you're ready to venture out on your own and create your own patterns, I think you'll be pleasantly surprised at how easy and straightforward it is. You probably have all of the supplies you need on hand already.

1. White paper (lined or plain)

2. Pencil

3. Eraser

4. Black felt-tip pen (or any black or dark marker)

5. Embroidery hoop in desired size

To begin, first decide which size and shape hoop you will be using for your design. Use your pencil to trace the inside of the hoop (not the outside) onto your piece of paper. This will act as your guide when you draw your pattern.

Lined or plain white paper both work perfectly. I tend to use lined paper when my pattern contains text, so it's straight, and unlined paper with everything else.

Using your pencil, begin to draw your pattern inside your traced hoop, making sure not to go all the way to the edges. We'll be erasing the pencil later, so this doesn't have to be perfect. Since you already traced your hoop, you know exactly how it will fit and be placed in the finished product. Once you're happy with your design, trace over it with your felt-tip pen or marker. Use your eraser to get rid of any pencil markings.

That's it! You've now got your very own custom pattern.

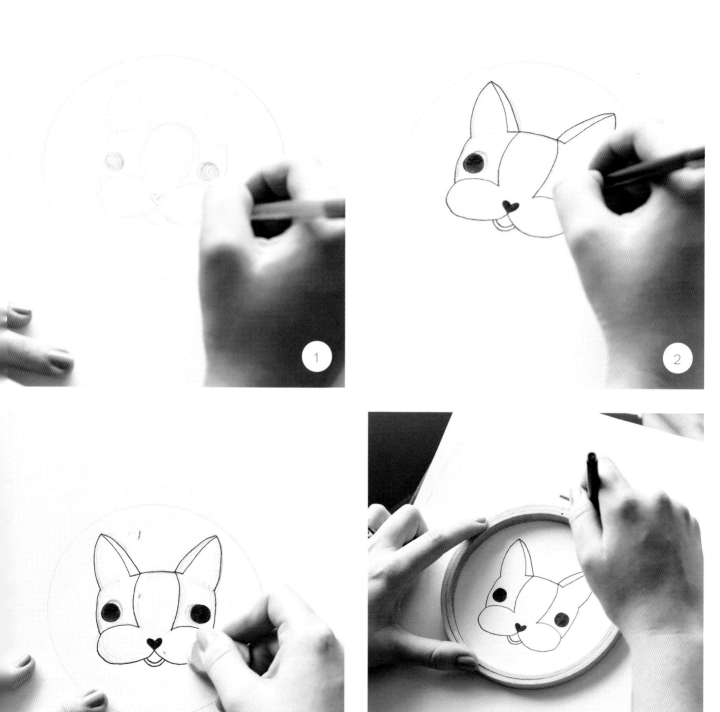

POISON BOTTLE

ANATOMICAL HEART

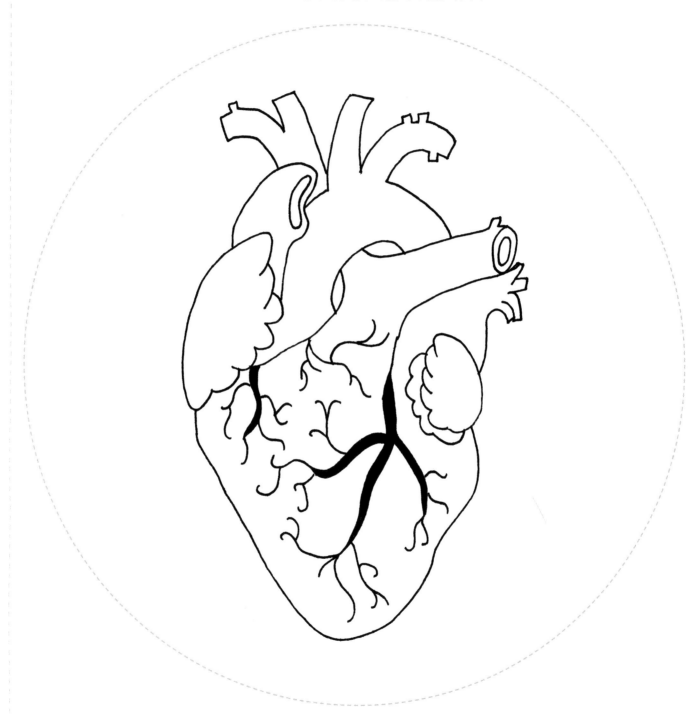

RIB CAGE

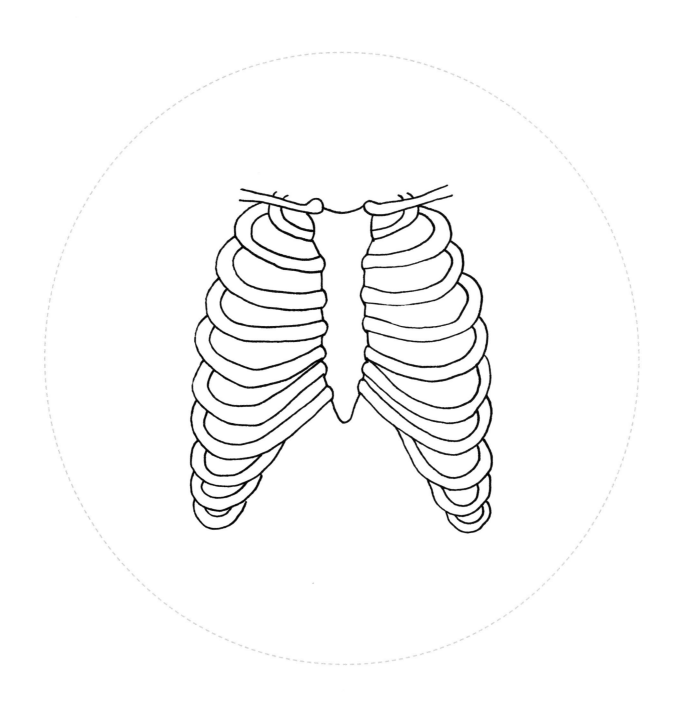

HAUNTED HOUSE
ON THE HILL

Figure 19

SHARP TEETH

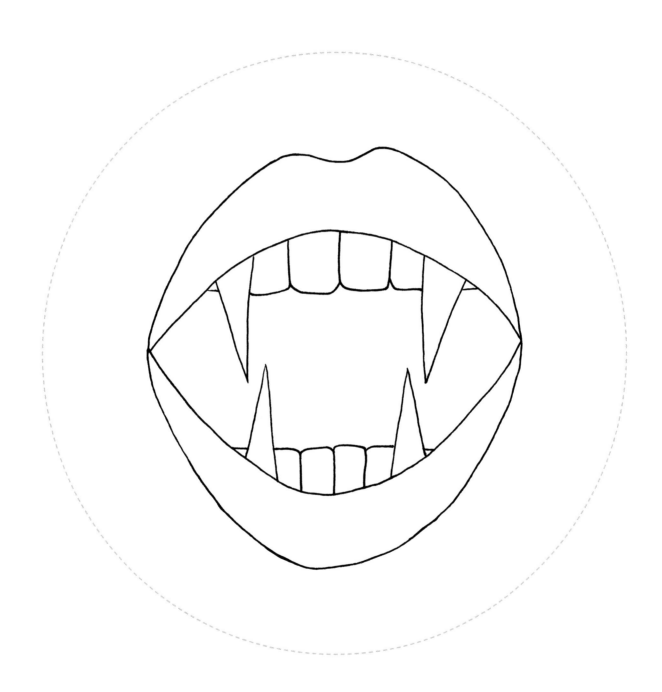

OUTER SPACE

DON'T BE A PRICK

GEOMETRIC SUCCULENT TERRARIUM

CANDY HEARTS

CRYSTAL BALL

CAN U NOT BANNER HEART

GHOULS NIGHT OUT

FERN SKULL

FALLING LEAVES

CONFETTI AMPERSAND

HANDFUL OF HYACINTHS

FLORAL BIRD SKULL

FLORAL SHARK ATTACK

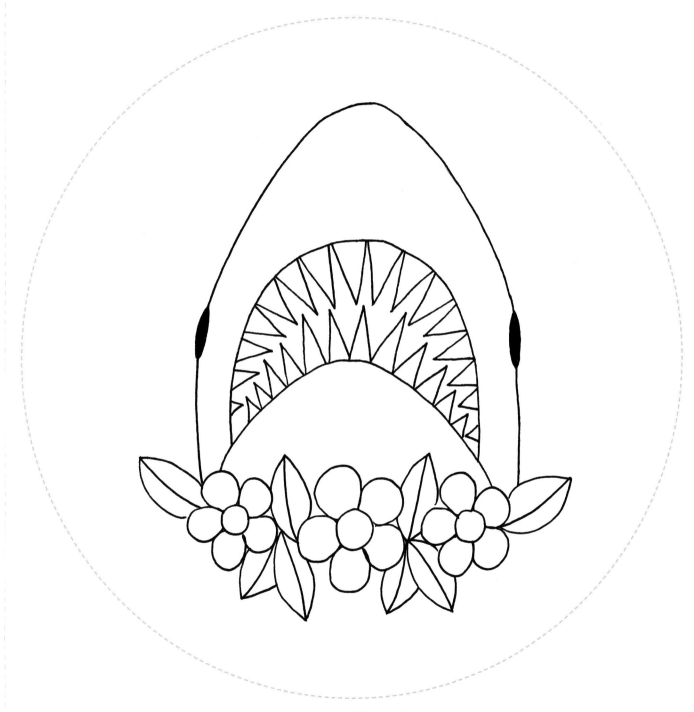

FINGERS CROSSED

GOOD LUCK

FLORAL CROWN COW SKULL

ACKNOWLEDGMENTS

I've been fortunate to be surrounded by a wonderful bubble of supportive folks both throughout my life and in the process of writing this book, and I'd like to thank them here.

First, I want to extend a huge thank-you to my editor, Lauren, and the rest of the fantastic team at Page Street for believing in the awesomeness of embroidery and guiding me along this journey. I literally could not have done this without you!

I would also like to extend my thanks and a whole bunch of love to my wonderful parents, Beth and Dave, who raised me to be the woman I am today and are my constant cheerleaders; my husband, James, who is the most supportive, patient and loving partner I could ever ask for; and last, but certainly not least, my grandmas, who taught me through example and practice the value of making things with your own hands, whether it's dollhouse miniatures or chocolate chip cookies.

ABOUT THE AUTHOR

Hi! I'm Renee. I've been running my embroidery business, MoonriseWhims, since 2014, after I decided it was time to make my own path and be my own boss. *Edgy Embroidery* is my first foray into both book writing and teaching.

I've always been crafty, but it wasn't until the early 2000s that I had a lightbulb moment and discovered my passion for hand embroidery. Over the years, I taught myself the art and developed my own techniques when I wasn't satisfied with what was out there. I can't imagine a life that doesn't include stitching every day.

I live in Southern California with my husband, our pair of Boston terriers and our cat. My passions in life, outside of embroidery, are often also rich sources of inspiration and include vintage shopping, reading and science fiction.

INDEX

See also back stitch; fern stitch; lazy daisy, satin stitch; stem stitch; straight stitch

straight stitch

Floral Border, 141

Floral Bird Skull, 68, 69, 143

flowers, how to make, 64, 65

Moonrise Roses, 78, 79, 80, 81

T

threading a needle, 12

tools

floss, 89–90

hoops, 93–94

needles, 89

organizing, 97–98

pattern making, DIY, 102, 103

pattern transfer tools, 92

scissors, 90, 92

transfer of pattern, 10, 11

W

washing finished embroidery, 99